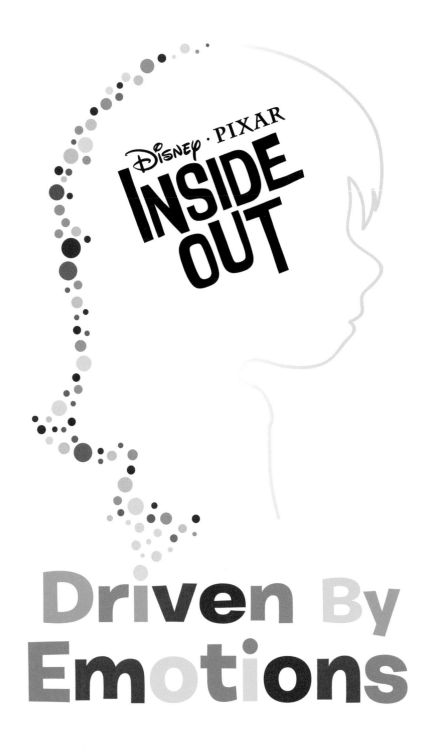

DISNEY · PIXAR

INSIDE OUT

Driven By
Emotions

Published by Disney Press, an imprint of Disney Book Group. No part of this book may be reproduced or transmitted in any form or by any means, electronic or mechanical, including photocopying, recording, or by any information storage and retrieval system, without written permission from the publisher. For information address Disney Press, 1101 Flower Street, Glendale, California 91201.

Printed in the United States of America
First Edition, May 2015
10 9 8 7 6 5 4 3 2

Library of Congress Control Number: 2014954384
FAC-008598-15212
ISBN 978-1-4847-2203-9

Visit www.disneybooks.com

Driven By Emotions

Five Stories Told from the Mind

by **Elise Allen**

Illustrated by **Jerrod Maruyama**

Designed by **Winnie Ho**

 PRESS

Los Angeles • New York

To my parents,
thank you for
letting me draw.
Jerrod

To Maddie,
all her emotions, and her
glorious islands of personality.
Love always,
Mom

Have you ever looked at someone and wondered what is going on inside their head? Well, I know what's going on in Riley's head. Mainly because I live inside it. I'm Joy, one of Riley's Emotions. There are five of us: me, Fear, Disgust, Anger, and Sadness. We've been with her from the very beginning: the minute she was born. We all hang out at Headquarters in Riley's head, where we take our turns at the control console. The console's like the dashboard of a spaceship, with all kinds of dials, knobs, wheels, and levers. We Emotions use the console to help Riley find the best ways to make the most out of each glorious day.

Did I say "we Emotions"? I did, didn't I?

Okay, well, the truth is that I have always been the one *really* in charge. Fear, Disgust, Anger, and Sadness are *super* great and *important*, but the main goal was always keeping Riley happy . . . which meant I drove the console most of the time. After all, why shouldn't Riley have been happy? She had super-fun parents who loved her like crazy; she had terrific friends like Meg; and she lived in Minnesota, which is only the coolest place ever to skate and play ice hockey and have the best time in the world!

So, for a long time, everything was great. Better than great—it was perfect.

Then something happened.

I'm not saying it was a horrible something. Of course not! But it was something, and it was pretty big.

When Riley was eleven, her family moved to San Francisco. Which is a *long* way from Minnesota.

Yes, I know—total big deal, very surprising, and not the best news in the world at first, but, hey—it didn't have to be a disaster. Oh, sure, the other Emotions had little panic attacks when we all found out, but I knew that if Mom and Dad were making this decision, there was a good reason, and we'd all be as happy in our new home as we were in the old one.

The move started out with a road trip, which, as you know, is the most fun way to spend several days. Yes, Riley was a little cramped sitting in the backseat forever, but you know what? It gave us *lots* of time to think about what our new house would look like! I was so excited to see it! I knew it would have balconies, and gables, and maybe even a moat we could cruise through in a speedboat . . .

As it turned out, the house wasn't *quite* like we imagined it. It was kind of small . . . and kind of dark . . . and it had the eensiest, *weensiest* little dead mouse in one corner . . . but it had *potential*! Once I saw Riley's room, I knew we could dress it up with her butterfly curtains, and her hockey lamp, and those supercool glow-in-the-dark stars we like to stick on the walls to make everything look like outer space. It would be amazing! All we had to do was get our stuff from the moving van and load it in.

Unfortunately, the moving van got lost on its way to San Francisco, and Riley wouldn't have her things for a few days. Everyone was upset: Fear, Anger, Disgust, and, of course, Sadness. Even Mom and Dad were frustrated and stressed out. But I had a stroke of genius! I grabbed a lightbulb and plugged it into the console, which is how Riley gets ideas. And you know what she did next? Our girl grabbed her hockey stick and threw a wad of crumpled-up paper on the empty living room floor, right near Mom and Dad.

"Andersen makes her move," Riley said. "She's closing in!"

Riley batted the paper around like a hockey puck, and the minute Dad saw it, he wanted to play, too!

"Oh, no, you're not," he said, grabbing a broom.

Soon Riley and Dad were skating all over the house, trying to score a goal in the empty fireplace.

"Come on, grandma!" Riley called to Mom.

"Ha!" Mom laughed. "'Grandma'?" Then she put up her hair and grabbed a pillow so she could play goalie. Now the whole family was skating across the floor on their socks, playing and laughing so hard they didn't even care about the missing furniture.

As the three of them played, a bright yellow sphere rolled into Headquarters.

It was a memory. A happy memory.

When things happen to Riley, new memories are made, and each memory is the color of its strongest emotion. Not to pat myself on the back or anything, but most of Riley's memories come in bright yellow. That's my color. It means her memories are joyful, just as they should be.

Since Riley does tons and tons of things, memories roll into Headquarters all day long. They fill up racks in the back, and at the end of the day, I make the announcement: "That's what I'm talking about—another perfect day! Nice job, everybody! Let's get those memories down to Long Term." Then we pull a lever that sends the spheres down to Long Term Memory for storage. When we want to help Riley remember something, we just call them back up again.

That's how it works for basic memories, but there are also core memories. Those are big-deal, life-altering events in Riley's life. The core memories are stored in the core memory holder—a very special place in Headquarters. Each core memory powers a different aspect of Riley's personality— parts of her that are so important they grow into their own *islands*. We can see them from the big glass windows in Headquarters. There's Goofball Island, Friendship Island, Family Island, Hockey Island, and Honesty Island. They're all amazing because they're the things that make Riley . . . Riley!

The memory that rolled in when the family played hockey on the floor was a great memory, but it wasn't a core memory.

The moment didn't last. Dad soon got a call and had to leave for work. So what did Sadness say?

"Oh, he doesn't love us anymore. That's sad."

A little overly dramatic, right? Then Sadness wanted to drive the console, which is always a bad idea. Whichever Emotion is driving is the one Riley's feeling the most. As I said, I like to drive. But sometimes it makes sense for someone else to take the wheel for a while. Fear keeps Riley safe; Disgust keeps Riley from being poisoned physically and socially; and Anger makes sure things stay fair.

But Sadness . . . I'm not actually sure what Sadness does. And I've checked, but there's no place else for her to go, so . . . she's good. We're all good. It's just best if she doesn't drive.

So when Sadness tried to drive the console after Dad left, I may have kinda sorta blocked her way a bit. But it's only because I was remembering a pizza place we saw in the neighborhood, and I wanted Riley to suggest it to Mom for lunch! It was a great idea, and way better than letting Sadness drive. I mean, really—who doesn't love pizza?

Well, it turned out we didn't love pizza. At least not San Francisco pizza, because it had broccoli on it, which, yes, is a little weird. Riley was disappointed, and soon the memories rolling in were all the colors except yellow, which I hated to see.

"What was your favorite part of the drive, Riley?" Mom asked on the walk home from the pizza place. She was talking about the cross-country road trip we had just gone on.

Good ol' Mom. Leave it to her to try to cheer up Riley with happy thoughts. It was a great plan, and I knew exactly what memory to pull from Long Term. I punched some buttons on the console, and a memory popped up and began to play on the projector. Now Riley would remember it, and all of us Emotions could watch it on Headquarters' big screen.

I have to tell you, that memory was *hilarious!* Riley and her parents had pulled off the highway to see this giant cement dinosaur on the side of the road—already funny, right? While Dad knelt down to take a picture of Riley and Mom in front of the dinosaur, the car started rolling away! Dad had forgotten to put on the emergency brake! The car rolled backward downhill until it slammed into another dinosaur. Its tail went right through the back windshield. Can you believe it?

We were laughing like crazy thinking about it: me, Disgust, Fear, Anger. Even Riley was laughing.

Until she wasn't.

All of a sudden—out of nowhere—Riley got quiet and sad. I turned around, and you know what I saw?

Sadness.

Sadness had her hands on the memory, and it was turning *blue!* A happy, joyful, golden-yellow memory was turning Sadness-colored *blue!* I grabbed the memory and tried to wipe away the blue, but it wouldn't change back to yellow. It would be blue forever. Whenever Riley thought about that time with the dinosaur, she wouldn't feel happy anymore. She'd feel sad.

I couldn't believe it. Nothing like that had ever happened before. When a memory is happy, it's supposed to stay happy.

I didn't like it one bit, but I didn't have time to think about it. Riley was sad and I needed to make her happy right away. I told Sadness to keep her hands off the memories and turned my attention back to Riley. She was walking toward some very steep stairs with a long railing.

Okay, I could work with that. One of Riley's favorite things was sliding down railings. This was a great opportunity to make her happy again! I saw Goofball Island start up as Riley sat down on the railing—perfect!

But instead of sliding, Riley got off the railing and walked down the stairs.

Walked! When she could have *slid!*

What was going on?

Then I heard something rolling on the floor behind me. I looked down, and what I saw was so unbelievable, I was sure I had to be imagining it.

"A core memory!" Fear cried.

Yes. A core memory. Sitting on the floor, out of its holder. We all knew what that meant. We ran to the window and saw Goofball Island go dark. Without the core memory in the core memory holder, Goofball could not be powered up. That's why Riley hadn't slid down the railing. The Goofball part of her was powered down.

At that moment, I noticed that the core memory holder was open, and Sadness was right next to it.

"Sadness!" I shouted. "What are you doing?"

"It looked like one was crooked," Sadness said, "so I opened it and then it fell out!"

I put the core memory back in place and Goofball Island whirred to life. Thank goodness. I looked back at the screen and saw that Riley had jumped onto the railing and was sliding down.

Then Sadness reached out again for one of the core memories and it started to turn blue!

"Whoa, whoa, *whoa*!" I said, grabbing her hand. "Sadness, you nearly touched a core memory. And when you touch them, we can't change them back!"

Sadness apologized and said she didn't know what had gotten into her, but obviously she was a disaster waiting to happen. That wasn't a *bad* thing; it was just something that needed to be handled. So I handled it. I gave her some mind manuals to read. Who doesn't love mind manuals? With titles like *Long Term Memory Retrieval, Volume 47,* you just know they have to be fascinating! Okay, maybe not fascinating, but they gave Sadness something to do. Plus, that corner with the mind manual shelves is far away from the memories. I have to keep them safe!

So that took care of Sadness for the moment, but by bedtime, she wasn't the only one having trouble. The move had been really hard on everyone, and even though I reminded them we'd been through worse, they didn't see it. Disgust couldn't get over the weird pizza, Fear was still freaking out about the missing moving van, and Sadness piped up that all of Riley's friends were far away and we'd never see them. Anger was so upset he wanted to shout that one curse word we knew. I was really struggling to keep them together, but then Mom came in to kiss Riley good night, and you know what she did? She *thanked* Riley. Mom was so proud of Riley for being *joyful* through the difficult move. She said, "You've stayed our happy girl. Your dad's under a lot of pressure, but if you and I can keep smiling, it would be a big help. We can do that for him, right?"

At that moment, I couldn't have been more proud. We had a higher purpose now—we needed to support Dad. Of course we could do that! I stepped up to the console and began driving.

Riley told Mom she'd definitely keep smiling.

"What did we do to deserve you?" said Mom, and she gave Riley a kiss good night.

The other Emotions agreed that Mom was right. And I was satisfied that we were all on the same page again . . . Team Happy!

After that, we were all tired. Sadness, Anger, Disgust, and Fear went to sleep, but I had Dream Duty, which meant I took the night shift. I sent all the day's memories down to Long Term for storage, then settled in to watch the show that the Dream Productions team had put together. It played on the big screen, the same one where we watch Riley's memories.

I'm a big fan of Dream Productions. They come up with some great shows—super original, real cutting-edge comedy, crazy action sequences. I have a whole list of favorites I call up from time to time. But that night's was *not* one of their best. It was, in fact, a nightmare about the new house, which was not okay at all. It was the last thing Riley needed after her day. So even though I'm not supposed to mess with dreams, I made an executive decision. I pulled the plug on the dream and called up a memory for Riley and me to watch while she slept. It was one of my favorites: the time when Riley showed off her skating moves to Mom and Dad. She did twirls and jumps—she was brilliant! And Mom and Dad were so proud; they smiled as they watched her. Riley was so happy she couldn't stop laughing.

I watched the memory all night long. I even skated with her, gliding in time with little Riley around Headquarters like it was a rink.

"Don't you worry," I told her. "I'm gonna make sure that tomorrow is another great day. I promise."

I meant that promise, too. The next day was the first day of school, and I had huge plans for how to make it the best day ever.

And what better way to start the best day ever

than with an accordion serenade? I have to say, I'm quite fabulous on the accordion. I don't play it so much as *hug* it. The melodious sound of my accordion made my fellow Emotions jump to their feet and emerge from the break room.

"Okay, first day of school!" I cheered. "Very, very exciting! I was up late last night figuring out a plan. Fear, I need a list of all the possible negative outcomes on the first day at a new school."

"Way ahead of you there," Fear said, writing on a notepad. "Does anyone know how to spell 'meteor'?"

"Disgust," I said, "make sure Riley stands out today . . . but also blends in."

"When I'm through, Riley will look so good the other kids will look at their own outfits and barf," Disgust assured me.

I told Anger to unload the Train of Thought, which had just arrived at Headquarters. It's an actual train that goes around the giant landscape of Riley's mind delivering daydreams, facts, opinions, lightbulb ideas, and memories. At the moment, it was delivering extra daydreams. I'd ordered them in case things got slow in class.

"Sadness," I then said, with excitement in my voice, "I have a super-important job just for you." I led her to a spot in the back of Headquarters and drew a chalk circle on the floor around her feet. "This is the Circle of Sadness," I said. "Your job is to make sure that all the Sadness stays inside of it."

She wasn't thrilled with the idea, but then again, when is she ever thrilled about anything? I knew it was a great plan.

As for me, I tasked myself with driving the console and making sure Riley stayed happy all day long. "All right, everyone," I cried out to my fellow Emotions, "fresh start! We are gonna have a good day, which will turn into a good week, which will turn into a good year, which will turn into a good *life*!"

Yep, I had everything in place. By the time this day was over, I was positive Riley would have people *clamoring* to be her best friend. She'd probably get thirty birthday party invitations. Forty, maybe!

The others weren't quite as sure as I was, especially when Riley's teacher made her stand up and introduce herself. Not a problem. I worked the console, and Riley stood up and smiled.

"My name is Riley Andersen," she said. "I'm from Minnesota. And now I live here."

Good. Charming. The other kids were loving her already!

Then the teacher asked for more information. She wanted to know about the weather. I knew Riley would have no problem with that one. She smiled and said, "Yeah, it gets pretty cold. The lake freezes over, and that's when we play hockey . . ."

As Riley told everyone about playing hockey with her best friend, Meg, I helped her out. I called up a memory of the whole family skating together and played it on the big screen. It was so beautiful I couldn't stop grinning.

"It's kind of a family tradition," Riley continued. "We go out on the lake almost every weekend."

Then, suddenly, the screen in Headquarters turned blue!

"Or we did, until we moved away," Riley said.

Wait. That shouldn't be happening. The screen shouldn't be blue. Riley shouldn't be sad. This was a *happy* memory!

I spun around to see the projector. There was Sadness, *with her hands on the memory sphere!*

"Sadness!" I snapped. "You touched a memory? We talked about this."

"Oh, yeah, I know," Sadness said. "I'm sorry."

Unbelievable! I sent her back to her Circle of Sadness and frantically pushed some buttons on the console to get the now *sad* memory out of the projector, but it wouldn't budge. And the longer it sat there, the more upset Riley got. Soon she wasn't even speaking. But she was still standing. In front of the whole class. About to cry! And as Disgust so helpfully pointed out, all the cool kids were whispering.

"Get it out of there, Joy!" Fear wailed.

He was right. I had to get the memory out of the projector, even if I had to do it by hand. I yanked and tugged, but it was stuck tight.

"Somebody help me," I said, and Fear, Anger, and Disgust grabbed hold of the sphere, too. At least, we had Fear at first. He gave up and ran around in a panic when Riley got so sad she started to sob. I looked up at the console and realized why. *Sadness was driving the console!* That was worse than her touching a memory! With Sadness at the controls, there was no possible way Riley could recover from this. I had to get Sadness off the console immediately! With a mighty tug, I finally yanked the blue memory out of the projector, then ran to Sadness and pulled her away.

But it was too late. With a *PING!* a blue memory sphere rolled into Headquarters.

Everyone stopped and stared.

"It's a core memory!" Fear said.

"But it's blue!" Disgust gasped.

They were both right. The memory was blue, and it rolled right toward the core memory holder.

This was not acceptable. Riley couldn't have a sad core memory. She *couldn't!* It would change who Riley was fundamentally! I lunged for the button to pop up the core memory holder. With the holder raised, the new memory hit the holder's side and couldn't go in. Success!

Now all I had to do was get this horrible blue core memory as far away from the core memory holder as possible. I pressed another button and lowered a vacuum tube from the ceiling—the same vacuum that sends Riley's daily memories to Long Term for storage. I knew the memory wouldn't cause Riley any trouble down there.

But before I could get the memory sphere in the vacuum, Sadness tried to grab the memory away! I couldn't believe it! She actually *wanted* to keep this blue core memory. I held the sphere tight, but so did Sadness. Surprisingly, she has a heck of a grip. I struggled to get the sphere away from her, but before I could, we bumped into the core memory holder.

All five core memories spilled out.

I think I stopped breathing.

"AHHHHHHHHHHH!" wailed Disgust, Fear, and Anger.

Through the window, we saw all the Islands of Personality go dark.

This was the biggest disaster ever. *Ever.* I stopped fighting Sadness for the blue memory sphere and scrambled to gather the five *yellow* core memories. Sadness held on to the blue one. She wanted to put it inside the core memory holder, but I wouldn't let her. I lunged at the blue memory, and it slipped out of Sadness's hands. I almost cried with relief as it got sucked up the vacuum tube to Long Term Memory. But then, suddenly, I slipped and *dropped the yellow core memories!* One of them rolled toward the vacuum tube.

"No!" I shouted.

I leaped to save it . . . and got pulled into the vacuum tube myself, along with all five of the yellow core memories!

The tube whooshed me straight up out of Headquarters! The core memories were zipping along with me. I managed to corral them together, but it wasn't easy. The fierce suction of the vacuum threatened to tear them away, but I kept them as close as I could.

As I rocketed through the tube, everything around me was a blur. I couldn't tell if I was going up or down. I didn't know where I'd land. And then, suddenly . . .

BLAM!

I landed in a large cart of memory spheres. I could feel the spheres pushing into my back. Then I heard a scream. It was Sadness. I guess she'd been sucked up by the vacuum, too, and now she was falling toward me.

THUMP!

Ignoring her, I began frantically digging through the memory spheres that we were sitting on top of. I'd lost track of the core memories when I fell. I needed to get them back to Headquarters. If Riley lost the core memories, the Islands of Personality would be stopped forever, and then where would she be? More important . . . *who* would she be?

"One . . . two . . . three . . . okay, got 'em," I said as I balanced the five memories in my arms.

I looked around. We were in the Mind World on the cliffs outside Long Term Memory. From there I could see all five Islands of Personality surrounding the giant tower of Headquarters, which seemed impossibly high and incredibly far away. The islands themselves were separated from each other, Headquarters, and the cliffs by the vast abyss of Riley's Memory Dump.

I jumped out of the cart and looked at Goofball Island. It was still completely dark. Sadness walked up behind me. "Riley's Islands of Personality. They're ALL down! This is bad," she said.

I assured her that we could fix it. "We just have to get back to Headquarters, plug the core memories in, and Riley will be back to normal."

"Riley has no core memories, no personality islands, and no—" Sadness suddenly gasped.

"Wha—what is it?" I asked.

"You! You're not in Headquarters. Without you, Riley can't be happy," said Sadness.

She was right. Riley would be miserable until I got back to Headquarters. There was no time to waste. We ran across the bridge that led to Goofball Island. When we made it to Goofball, we came to the lightline that connected the island to the core memory holder in Headquarters. The lightline was like a power cord, and it was also our ticket back home! We just had to walk across it. Easier said than done.

Sadness didn't like the look of that lightline. Honestly, I couldn't blame her. It was super thin, and if we fell from it, we'd end up in the Memory Dump—forgotten forever. I summoned all of my courage. "It's not that high. It's totally fiii-fine." I took my first step out onto the lightline and nearly dropped one of the core memories! "Whoa . . . whoa!"

Sadness inched her way out on the lightline after me.

Suddenly, I heard an awful mechanical groan, unbelievably loud. I turned around, but what I saw seemed so impossible I almost didn't believe it.

Goofball Island had started to crumble.

As I stared, huge sections of it broke off and

crashed down into the Memory Dump. Then the lightline started to collapse, too! There was no way we were going to make it to Headquarters.

"AHHHH! Go back! Run! Run! Run!" I yelled at Sadness.

We ran as fast as we could back to the island, but it was disappearing faster now. We poured on the speed, ducking and dodging to avoid pieces of the collapsing island. We zoomed across the last remains of Goofball, tore over the bridge, and leaped back to the cliffs. Still, we weren't safe. Goofball's collapse made the cliffs unstable. I felt the ground slipping under my feet.

"Come on, Sadness!" I screamed as I grabbed her arm. "Run!"

She stumbled after me, and we made it to a more stable area just as the bridge and *all* of Goofball Island gave a final groan, collapsing into the emptiness below.

As I watched the island sink like a lost iceberg, images of the Goofball part of Riley's personality flashed in my mind. I saw her at three years old, giggling and spinning around until she fell. I saw her on Dad's shoulders, giving herself a cotton candy beard. I saw the whole family making silly faces at each other while they jumped on a trampoline.

That was all gone now. Riley would never have goofy times like that again.

No. That wasn't true. Riley would get Goofball back. I just had to return the core memories to the holder, and Goofball would grow back. Riley needed me to stay positive and take action, so I got to my feet and started marching.

"Wait, Joy, you could get lost in there!" Sadness said. She raced to catch up and grabbed my arm.

I looked ahead. Shelves stretched into the distance as far as the eye could see and towered overhead. They branched off into corridor after corridor of more shelves, each of which looked exactly like the others.

Sure, yes, it looked a little daunting, but I was determined, and I was positive, and I knew I'd be able to handle it without a problem!

"Think positive!" I told Sadness.

"Okay. I'm positive you will get lost in there. That's Long Term Memory. I read about it in the manual," she replied.

The manual! Of course! All that reading Sadness did while standing in her Circle of Sadness in Headquarters was finally going to pay off. "Congratulations! You are the Official Mind Map!" I exclaimed. "Lead on, Mind Map!"

"Okay," Sadness said, flopping down. "Only, I'm too sad to walk. Just give me a few . . . hours."

Since she refused to get up and join me, I grabbed her leg and dragged her into the shelving maze. "Which way? Left?" I asked.

"Right."

I turned right.

"No, I mean go left. I said left was right. Like 'correct.'"

Why was everything so complicated with Sadness?

I followed her directions and dragged her until, suddenly, everything went dark.

"Oh, Riley's gone to sleep," Sadness said.

"Okay." I perked up. "Then nothing else can happen! By the time she wakes up, I'll be back at Headquarters with the core memories."

That's what I thought. But by the time Riley woke up, we were *still* trudging through Long Term. Riley has a *lot* of memories.

I admit it, I was starting to get frustrated. I hadn't given up hope, no siree, but being lost with Sadness while Riley's entire personality was on the line . . . it was challenging. So when I heard voices up ahead, I dropped Sadness's leg and raced to find them.

It was two Mind Workers, and they were doing something with a vacuum cleaner, a clipboard, and some of Riley's memories.

"Phone numbers?" the first Mind Worker said. "She doesn't need those. They're in her phone."

"Forget it!" the other worker replied.

And they sucked several of Riley's memory spheres into the vacuum. To *forget* them! These weren't just any Mind Workers, they were Forgetters—Mind Workers; who worked in Long

Term Memory vacuuming up old memories. I had never heard of them before, but apparently they had been around a long time.

"Hey!" I shouted. "You can't throw those away! Those are perfectly good memories."

"Really," one Forgetter clucked. "The names of every *Cutie Pie Princess* doll?"

"Yes!" I shot back. "That is critical information! Glitterstorm, Honeypants, Officer Justice . . ."

"Forget 'em!" the other Forgetter cried, and then the first one vacuumed them up!

"Hey!" I objected. "Bring those back!"

"They're in the dump," the Forgetter replied. "Nothing comes back from the dump."

"When Riley doesn't care about a memory, it fades," said the other Forgetter.

"Fades?" I asked.

"Happens to the best of 'em," the Forgetter noted.

Wow. I had always thought when Riley made a memory, she had it forever. It was a shame any memory would fade away. The idea almost made me sad.

"This one will never fade," said the Forgetter, chuckling, as he removed a sphere from the shelf.

"The song from the gum commercial?" I asked. Of all memories to keep, that was the most ridiculous and useless one!

The Forgetters explained that they liked to send it to Headquarters for no reason. They began to play it over and over again.

"We all know the song. Okay, okay. Real catchy," I said.

Then one of the Forgetters replaced the memory on the shelf and tipped it backward. The memory got sucked up by a tube and sent straight to Headquarters.

I'm sure Anger, Disgust, and Fear really appreciated that.

I asked the Forgetters if they knew where I could find Friendship Island, but before they could answer, we all heard a terrible groaning noise. I followed the sound, running as fast as I could. What else was going wrong inside Riley's mind? I turned a corner and stopped in my tracks.

Friendship Island was crumbling to pieces!

"Oh, not Friendship Island," I said.

"Riley loved that one. And now it's gone," said Sadness. Apparently she'd caught up to me. If it was up to her, we'd just sit against a shelving unit and mope, but that is not my style. Friendship Island might be gone—for the moment—but I could see Hockey Island in the distance, and I was sure once we got there, we could get to Headquarters. We'd have to go back through Long Term to find a bridge to Hockey, but if that's what we needed to do, that's what we'd do.

CLONK.

The noise rang out somewhere behind us. I turned and saw a huge pink elephant humming to himself as he picked memory spheres off the Long Term shelves.

I walked right up to him. "Hello!" I said.

The elephant froze for a moment and then sprinted off!

"Wait! Hey! Wait!" I yelled.

But the elephant wouldn't stop. He just kept on

running! We followed him around a corner and into a dead end. He frantically tried to climb a wall, but he wasn't getting anywhere.

"Um, excuse me?" I said.

"AHHHHHHHH!" he screamed. He then grabbed a memory sphere from one of the shelves, throwing it in one direction and taking off in the other. After that he ran right into a cart of memories!

"Are you okay?" I asked him.

"I don't think so," he replied.

There was something familiar about this odd creature. He looked like a pink elephant, but he also had a big, fluffy cat's tail, and . . .

"Hey, I know you! You're Bing Bong! Riley's imaginary friend! Riley loved playing with you. You two were the best of friends." Then it dawned on me. Bing Bong could help us! "Oh! You would know! We're trying to get back to Headquarters . . ."

"You guys are from Headquarters?" asked Bing Bong.

I nodded. "I'm Joy, and this is Sadness."

"Joy? THE Joy?" asked Bing Bong.

I couldn't help but feel a little flattered. Apparently I was famous in the Mind World!

Bing Bong suddenly realized that if I was in the Mind World and not in Headquarters, Riley would never be happy. "We gotta get you back," he said. "I tell you what . . . follow me!"

"Oh, thank you!" I cried.

As Sadness and I followed Bing Bong down a row of memory spheres, we began reminiscing about all the great times Bing Bong had with Riley. There was the time when they were in a band together, and the time when they played tag. But they had their best adventures in Bing Bong's rocket. I remembered his rocket ran on song power! And not just any song . . . Bing Bong's theme song that Riley wrote! Oh, those were the best times.

A dull voice interrupted our reminiscing. It was Sadness. "What exactly are you supposed to be?" she asked.

"You know," Bing Bong replied, "it's unclear. I'm part cat . . . part elephant . . . part dolphin."

I looked him over. I didn't see any dolphin bits. "Dolphin?" I asked.

He plugged his elephant trunk and made a noise *exactly* like a dolphin's. It was pretty impressive. "What are you doing out here?" I asked him.

"Well," he said, "there's not much call for imaginary friends lately. So, uh, you know, I'm . . ."

"Hey, hey, don't be sad," I said. "When I get back up to Headquarters, I'll make sure Riley remembers you!"

"You will?" he asked, suddenly perking up.

"Of course! She'd love that!"

"Ha, ha! This is the greatest day of my life!" Bing Bong cried. He then started doing a little jig, which ended with him getting hurt. He began to cry, and candy tears poured out of his eyes.

"What's going on?" asked Sadness.

"I cry candy," said Bing Bong. "Try the caramel, it's delicious."

Mmmmm! I reached out for one, but the five memory spheres I was holding began to slip.

"Oh, here, use this," said Bing Bong, emptying

out the satchel he was carrying. Everything from a kitchen sink to a cat came tumbling out! Sadness and I stared at Bing Bong in amazement.

"What? It's imaginary," said Bing Bong, and he handed the satchel to me.

"Thanks," I said, slipping the memories inside. "This'll make it a lot easier to walk back to Headquarters."

"Walk?" Bing Bong said. "We're not walking! We're taking the Train of Thought!"

Yes! The Train of Thought! I couldn't believe I hadn't thought of it! I'd used it just the other day to get those extra daydreams for the first day of school. The train ran from down here to Headquarters all the time!

"How do we catch it?" I asked.

"Well," Bing Bong said, "it kind of goes all over the place, but there is a station in Imagination Land. I know a shortcut. Come on, this way!"

Sadness and I followed Bing Bong through Long Term Memory until we came to a building that appeared to be some kind of warehouse or factory. When I looked through its window, I saw out the other side—and there was the train station!

No wonder Riley had loved Bing Bong so much when she was little. He was brilliant!

"After you," he said, opening the door.

Sadness grabbed my arm. "I read about this place in the manual," she said. "We shouldn't go in there. This is Abstract Thought. Let's go around."

Leave it to Sadness to be negative. I looked to see how far it would be to go around. The answer? *Super* far! The building was huge! There was absolutely no good reason we shouldn't listen to Bing Bong and take the shortcut.

"Look," I told Sadness, "we don't want to miss the train. Bing Bong knows what he's doing. He's part dolphin. They're very smart!"

I gave her my happiest, most joyfully positive smile, and it worked. Sadness followed Bing Bong and me into the building. Score! Soon we'd be on the train and on our way back to Headquarters!

Soon after we walked into the Abstract Thought building, the door slammed shut behind us.

Unexpected, but nothing to worry about.

Then all kinds of shapes floated up from the floor: little triangles and circles and rectangles of various sizes and colors. It was like standing inside a kaleidoscope. So beautiful.

Then the shapes began to melt in a weird, goopy kind of way.

"What's happening?" I asked.

"Oh, no," said Sadness, as she shuddered. "They turned it on."

"I've never seen this before," Bing Bong said.

I turned to look at him. His face had changed! It was all flat and blocky! I screamed, and when Bing Bong looked at me, he screamed, too.

I looked at Sadness. She had changed, as well! Then I carefully raised my hands toward my own face. I felt my nose sticking out two feet beyond my face. It was flat and pointed.

"AAAAAAH!" I screamed. "What is going on?"

"We're abstracting!" Sadness cried. "There are four stages. This is the first: nonobjective fragmentation!"

I had no idea what that meant. I only knew we needed to get out of the building. I tried to run, but my legs were stiff boards without knees. And my arms couldn't pump, because my elbows were gone.

"Oh!" I wailed. "What do we do?"

"All right, do not panic!" Bing Bong advised. "What is important is that we all *stay together!*"

Then his arm fell off.

It was time to panic. I would have tried to run again, but my head popped off. Then Sadness's leg fell off, causing her to tumble to the floor.

"We're in the second stage," Sadness explained. "We're deconstructing!"

Pulling ourselves together—literally—we raced for the window. Oddly enough, it's difficult to move quickly when you're juggling your own body pieces. Just saying.

"We've gotta get out of this place before we're nothing but shape and color and get stuck here forever!" Sadness cried.

Then things got worse. We deflated into

two-dimensional shapes. Have you ever tried to move when you're as flat as a pancake? I don't recommend it. That was apparently stage three. We all still struggled for the window, but it seemed to get farther and farther away.

POP!

We abstracted into flat blobs.

"Oh, no!" Sadness groaned. "We're non-figurative. This is the last stage!"

I didn't want to give up. I'm *not* a giver-upper. But what were we going to do?

"Wait!" Sadness suddenly shouted. "We're two-dimensional. Fall on your face!"

She fell forward. Instead of a blob of color, she was now a line and crawled inchworm-like toward the window.

It was brilliant! Bing Bong and I did the same, and we made it out the window . . . just as the train pulled away without us. We tried to run after it, but it took a while for us to get back to our regular shapes. By the time we did, the train was long gone.

"Don't worry, there's another station. That way!"

Driven By Emotions

said Bing Bong, pointing off into the distance. "The train always stops there right before it goes to Headquarters. If we hurry, we can catch it!"

After what we had just been through, I wasn't sure we should rely on Bing Bong to point us in the right direction anymore.

"This isn't another one of your shortcuts, is it?" I asked him.

"Ha, ha, ha! Yeah!" he said, and walked off.

I turned to Sadness. "Is there really another station?"

Sadness nodded yes. "Through there," she said.

Sadness knew her way around—I trusted her. So we followed Bing Bong, and soon enough we were at the gates of . . .

"Imagination Land!" exclaimed Bing Bong. "I come here all the time. I'm practically the mayor!"

Bing Bong first took us through French Fry Forest, which was absolutely finger-licking good! The fries were crispy on the outside, soft on the inside, hot enough to be delicious without burning your tongue . . . perfection.

Then we went through Trophy Town, which was just filled with trophies and medals. Bing Bong saw a soccer ball on the ground and kicked it into a goal, and workers *swarmed* out to load his arms with trophies and flower bouquets and hang medals around his neck. So fun!

And then I saw *Cloud Town*! For real—a town made of clouds! I pulled a small chunk of cloud off a building and jumped on as it floated into the air. It was so soft!

Bing Bong then headed to the House of Cards—an actual house made of playing cards—and emerged with his rocket. Well, it was really a wagon, but when he played with Riley, it transformed into a rocket that took them on the most amazing adventures!

"I stashed it in there for safekeeping," said Bing Bong. "Now I'm all set to take Riley to the moon!" Then he accidentally bumped into the House of Cards, and it collapsed. "Oh, I'm sorry," he said.

"Great," muttered a construction worker.

"I love Imagination Land," I said.

"Isn't it great?" he replied. "And there's always something new, like . . . who the heck is that?"

Bing Bong was looking at a giant machine with a conveyer belt. A teenage boy with hair flopping in his face, dark brown eyes, and a major case of bad-boy attitude rolled out onto the belt.

"Imaginary boyfriend," said a nearby worker.

When the boy turned to look at us, we could see the depths of heartsick despair in his gaze. "I would die for Riley," he said.

Ewww.

We quickly moved beyond the Imaginary Boyfriend Generator.

"This way, through Preschool World! We're nearly to the train!" said Bing Bong.

Sadness and I followed Bing Bong to the Preschool World gates. Just then, there was a loud *BOOM!* I quickly turned around and saw Hockey Island collapsing. Riley loved hockey! She couldn't give up on hockey.

I knelt down and pulled out Riley's hockey core memory from the satchel. The memory sphere showed Riley when she was just two-and-a-half years old. She was with Mom and Dad on the frozen lake, trying to shoot a puck into the goal. She missed at first but then spun around and accidentally knocked the puck into the goal. She was so proud of herself, and so were Mom and Dad. I looked up at the empty space where Hockey Island used to be. I sighed and then quickly caught up with Bing Bong.

"We have to get to that station," I told him.

"Sure thing," he said. "This way, just past Graham Cracker Castle."

But there was no Graham Cracker Castle. Bing Bong looked confused. "It used to be right here. And where's . . . I could have sworn Sparkle Pony Mountain was right over there. What's going on?"

Just then, a bulldozer came by and knocked over a cotton candy-pink castle.

"Princess Dream World!" Bing Bong gasped.

The bulldozer kept knocking things over. Soon the air was so full of glitter and fluff that I could barely breathe. What was this stuff?

"The Stuffed Animal Hall of Fame!" Bing Bong wailed. Then he screamed out loud, "My rocket!"

He ran as fast as he could, chasing two Mind Workers who had taken his rocket when he wasn't looking. Bing Bong tried to catch up to them, but they were faster and they had a head start. They tossed the wagon onto a pile of rubble that was getting bulldozed off a cliff.

"Wait!" Bing Bong pleaded. "Riley and I were still using that rocket! It still has some song power left!" He sang his theme song and the rocket fired forward, powered by the music.

Unfortunately, when it zipped forward, it launched itself over the cliff and into the dump below. Bing Bong fell to his knees.

"Riley can't be done with me," he murmured.

I hated to see him so sad, especially when we had a mission to accomplish that would put everything back to normal. I put a hand on his back and tried to rally him. "We can fix this!" I assured him. "We just need to get back to Headquarters. Which way to the train station?"

"I had a whole trip planned for us," Bing Bong said sadly.

He was *not* snapping out of it. I had to try a new tactic. "Hey, who's ticklish, huh? Here comes the tickle monster . . ."

I tickled him under his arms, which is the most supremely ticklish part of the entire body, but he didn't even move. Not a giggle, not a flinch.

"Hey, Bing Bong!" I tried. "Look at this!"

I made the goofiest face in my arsenal: crossed eyes, tongue out, fingers pulling my lips wide apart in two different directions.

No response at all. How was I going to make him happy again so he could lead us to the train station?

Then Sadness came over and plopped down beside him.

"I'm sorry they took your rocket," she said gently. "They took something that you loved. It's gone . . . forever."

Oh, great. That's just what Bing Bong needed—something to make him feel even worse.

"It's all I had left of Riley," Bing Bong said.

"I bet you and Riley had great adventures," Sadness said, once again reminding him how much he'd lost. Honestly, she does not understand how to be *positive!*

"They were wonderful," Bing Bong agreed. "Once we flew back in time. We had breakfast twice that day."

"That sounds amazing," Sadness said. "I bet Riley liked it."

"Oh, she did," Bing Bong said. "We were best friends."

Then Bing Bong started to cry. His candy tears weren't so bad . . . actually, they were kind of delicious . . . but still! What was Sadness thinking? Why had she made him cry?

"Yeah, it's sad," Sadness said.

Bing Bong put his head on Sadness's shoulder, and the candy tears started to pour.

Sadness kept her arm around him while he cried. Eventually, he sat back up, sniffling and blinking.

"I'm okay now. C'mon, the train station is this way," said Bing Bong.

My jaw dropped open. How did that happen? How did *crying* motivate Bing Bong to help us get back to Headquarters? As Sadness and I followed him, I pulled her aside and asked, "How did you do that?"

"I don't know," Sadness said. "He was sad. So I listened—"

"Hey!" Bing Bong shouted. "There's the train!"

Sadness and I ran to catch up with him. The Train of Thought was right there at the station, and we climbed aboard just as it started up. We were on our way, and everything was going to work out perfectly.

At least, it *would have* worked out perfectly if the train hadn't stopped when we were only halfway through the long ride to Headquarters.

"Hey, hey!" I called to the engineer. "Why aren't we moving?"

"Riley's gone to sleep," the engineer said. "We're all on break."

"Oh, yeah," Bing Bong remembered. "The Train of Thought doesn't run while she's asleep."

"You mean we're stuck here until morning?" Sadness wailed.

"We can't wait that long!" I said. But a second later, I had a great idea—we could wake Riley up! Or maybe Sadness had the idea, but I don't think so. I think it was mine. Either way, it doesn't matter. The main thing is the idea was terrific. So Sadness, Bing Bong, and I got off the train and walked onto the lot of Dream Productions. I was super excited. Like I said, I'd *always* been a huge fan of Dream Productions, and there I was! I saw lots of big studio buildings, actors walking around in costumes, golf carts zipping this way and that. I even recognized the guy who played Riley's hockey coach in her favorite recurring Olympics dream!

Then it got even better. I saw a giant white horse-creature with a pink horn. She sat in a director's chair sipping a latte. I grabbed Bing Bong's arm. "Rainbow Unicorn! She's *right there!*"

I didn't want to make a big fuss and embarrass

her, so I just gave her a little nod as we walked by, but Sadness went right up to her.

"My friend says you're famous," she said. "She wants your autograph."

Again with the embarrassing! I pulled Sadness away and kept on walking—but not before Rainbow Unicorn and I had a great moment together, where I told her how amazing she was and she really appreciated it. We're definitely friends now.

Soon we came to a large building that said STAGE B. There was a red flashing light on the building and a sign that said DO NOT ENTER WHEN LIGHT IS FLASHING.

"Huh," Bing Bong said. "Wonder what that means. Ah well, let's go in."

We went into the room and it looked so exciting! People were running everywhere, working cameras, carrying script pages, focusing lights. It was show business in action! Sadness, Bing Bong, and I hid behind a costume rack as we decided what to do. "How are we gonna wake her up?" I asked.

"Well," Sadness said, "she wakes up sometimes

when she has a scary dream. We could scare her."

That was a terrible idea. Why make Riley feel terrified when we could make her feel happy? "We are going to make Riley so happy that she'll wake up with exhilaration," I suggested. "We'll excite her awake!" I looked through the costume rack and found a dog costume. It had two pieces—one for the back half and one for the front. I tossed Sadness the back half of the costume. "Put this on," I told her. "Riley loves dogs!"

I gave Bing Bong the bag of core memories to hold. "Don't let anything happen to these," I told him. Then I tossed on the top half of the dog costume and led Sadness to the side of the set. It was set up like a classroom, and when the scene started, I knew what they were doing—acting out Riley's first day of school, when she cried in front of everyone.

Who writes these scripts? Why would they show that to Riley when it was hard enough going through it in real life? Good thing I was on the scene to make things happier.

I waited until the most dramatic point of the scene, when Riley was standing in front of everyone, and then Sadness and I loped onto the set. We pranced around just like a real puppy! I barked, we trotted in circles, I made the puppy's tongue lick Riley and all the other students . . . I was *adorable*! No way Riley could resist this. Sure, it's true, the dial on the wall said Riley was still asleep, but she couldn't stay asleep for much longer. Not with this much fun going on, right?

And it was about to get even better. I looked at Bing Bong, who was watching from backstage. "*Psst!* You're on! Go!" Bing Bong pulled a rope that let a ton of balloons fall from the ceiling, and another rope that set off a confetti cannon. Now it was a puppy dance party! Riley would spring awake and start dancing!

"Joy, this isn't working," Sadness said from the back half of the dog, but I didn't listen. I was dancing, Bing Bong was dancing . . . this was irresistibly fun!

Then Bing Bong danced into a light . . . that crashed onto the stage . . . that made Sadness jump away from me—which made it look like the adorable puppy had split in half!

Then there was chaos. Actors were running around to avoid the fallen light, technicians were trying to shoo Sadness and I offstage, and Bing Bong decided that was the perfect time to speak directly to Riley and get them to be friends again.

"Hi, Riley, it's me! BING BONG!"

"Joy, look!" Sadness said. "It's working!"

There was *nothing* working about it. At least, that's what I thought. But when I looked where Sadness was pointing, I saw the dial on the wall had moved! Riley was slowly getting closer to awake! Soon we'd be able to get out of there and hop back on the Train of Thought!

"They're trying to wake her up!" the director said, pointing to Bing Bong, Sadness, and me. "Call security!"

Sadness and I ducked away and hid, but Bing Bong wasn't as fast. A security guard put him in handcuffs and dragged him away. We watched from the shadows as the guard pulled Bing Bong out of the studio and threw him through a thick, scary gate into a dark pit of a chamber. We heard Bing Bong's screams getting softer and softer as he sunk down into the depths.

"They threw him into the Subconscious," Sadness said. "I read about it in the manual. It's where they take all the troublemakers."

"He has the core memories," I told Sadness. "We have to go after him."

Luckily, Sadness knew the way. We walked down as everything around us grew dim and then dark. Finally, we made it to another gate. Two guards were standing nearby, but they were deep in conversation, so Sadness and I simply snuck past them and walked right up to the gate. Sadness rattled it and the guards spun around.

"Hey! You!" one shouted.

"Oh! You caught us!" Sadness said as if she was really upset about it.

"Get back in there!" the other guard demanded. "No escaping!"

The two of them shoved us into the

Subconscious and slammed the gate behind us.

Okay, so we were in there with Bing Bong and the core memories. We just had to find him, get the memories, get *out* of the Subconscious, then catch the Train of Thought back to Headquarters. Easy peasy!

"I don't like it here," Sadness said. "It's where they keep Riley's darkest fears."

It was true. I tried to be brave, but horror after horror leaped out of the darkness and lunged at us. Terrors like broccoli, the stairs to the basement, and Grandma's vacuum cleaner. My heart was pounding so hard I could barely breathe, but I pulled it together and made sure Sadness did the same. We tiptoed forward so we wouldn't attract the attention of anything scary, but every step we took crunched.

"Would you walk quieter?" I hissed.

"I'm trying!" she whispered back.

Then I looked down to see what was so noisy, and I saw them.

Candy wrappers.

From an imaginary friend who cried candy? I suspected yes. We followed the wrapper trail and found Bing Bong. He was in a jail cell . . . made of balloons.

"There you are!" I cried.

"Shhhh!" Bing Bong warned me. He pointed downward. His jail cell was on the belly of a giant sleeping clown!

I recognized the clown and shuddered. He was the entertainment at Riley's cousin's birthday party a long time ago. His face was deathly white; horrible blue stars marked his beady, evil eyes; and his mouth spread in an inhumanly large red grin. He must have been ten times the size he was in real life, and just as terrifying.

"Jangles," I whispered, my voice quivering.

"Who's the birthday girl? Who's the birthday girl?" the clown repeatedly murmured in his sleep. His bright blue curls fluttered every time he exhaled.

"Do you have the core memories?" I asked Bing Bong.

He handed them to me and I hugged them close. Thank goodness they were safe!

"All he cared about was the candy," Bing Bong said softly. "Then he twisted this balloon cage and locked me inside."

I had to help Bing Bong escape. I pulled apart the bars of the balloon cage, but they SQUEEEAKED so horribly I was sure Jangles would wake up. We froze as the giant clown snuffled and snorted . . . but soon he was breathing deeply again, and we eased Bing Bong out. We were free to go, but just as we started to run away, I realized something. *Wait. The train's not running.* I stopped and turned to Sadness. "We still have to wake up Riley," I said.

"But how?" asked Sadness.

We looked back at the clown and knew what we had to do.

"Oh, no," muttered Bing Bong.

We walked right up to Jangles and honked his nose. The clown's eyes popped open. He stood up, towering over me until I felt tiny like an ant.

"H-hey, Sadness, di-did you hear about the p-pahh-party that we're having?" I said.

"Ohhhh, yeah. Yes, Joy! Isn't it a ba-bahh-birthday party?" said Sadness.

"Did you say . . . birthday?" Jangles leered.

"Yes!" I assured him. "And there's going to be cake and presents and—"

"And games and balloons—" added Sadness.

"A BIRTHDAY?" Jangles roared. He pulled out a mallet large enough to flatten me with one stroke.

"Okay!" I encouraged him. "Follow us!"

I ran as fast as I could, Sadness and Bing Bong right behind me. We raced all the way to the gates of the Subconscious. Jangles bashed down the gates with his mallet, terrifying the guards, who ran away and didn't try to stop us. We ran all the way back to the Dream Productions set, where I pointed Jangles toward the outside wall.

Jangles demolished the wall with his mallet, then leaned into the camera with his wickedly toothy smile. "WHO'S THE BIRTHDAY GIRL?" he roared.

I saw the dial flip immediately to AWAKE. Riley was up!

"Woo-hoo!" I yelled.

Sadness and I did a little happy dance. Mission accomplished!

"Come on, let's go!" said Bing Bong.

We sprinted to the Train of Thought, leaving quite a ruckus behind us. Jangles was laughing maniacally while smashing up the sets. Worst nightmare ever!

When we got to the train, it was already moving at full speed. We ran as fast as we could and leaped aboard the last car.

"Ha, ha! We made it! Guess who's on their way to Headquarters?" I exclaimed, grabbing Sadness and swinging her around in celebration.

"We are!" said Sadness.

Once we were all settled on the train, tucked in among the memories heading up to Headquarters, I turned to Sadness. "That was a good idea," I admitted, "about scaring Riley awake. You're not so bad."

"Really?" Sadness said.

"Nice work," I said.

Bing Bong had picked up one of the memory spheres that was being transported in the train. It was the twisty-tree memory—one of my favorites! Riley had just finished playing hockey and was standing beside that big twisty tree near the lake, when her whole hockey team showed up and started cheering for her. Mom and Dad were there cheering, too . . . Riley was so happy and laughing. I loved it.

"Whoa, is this Riley?" Bing Bong asked.

I nodded. I forgot he hadn't played with Riley since she was three.

"She's so big now, she won't fit in my rocket," Bing Bong said. "How are we going to get to the moon?"

Sadness had been looking at the memory, too. "I remember that day," she said. "I love that one."

I couldn't believe it. Sadness actually liked a happy memory? "Atta girl!" I cried excitedly. "Now you're getting it!"

"Yeah," Sadness sighed. "It was the day the Prairie Dogs lost the big play-off game. Riley missed the winning shot. She felt awful. She wanted to quit."

Sadness noticed my face fall. "Sorry," she said. "I can't help it."

"I'll tell you what. We'll keep working on it together. Okay?"

Sadness agreed with a weak smile.

I slipped the twisty-tree memory into the satchel with the core memories. I thought it would be great to have it around Headquarters. I daydreamed about how wonderful it would be to return to Headquarters and put everything back to normal, but then I heard a horrible CREAK. The entire train shuddered. I spun around and saw Honesty Island crumble and sink into nothingness!

"NO!" I screamed, but my voice was swallowed by more creaking and squealing as the crumbling island shook everything around us so violently that the entire Train of Thought plummeted off its track!

Bing Bong, Sadness, and I screamed as the train

fell. We crashed and fell among the cliffs of Riley's mind . . . landing right back where we'd started.

"That was our way home!" I wailed. "We lost another island . . . what is happening?"

Then one of the workers who had come to clean up after the crash said, "Haven't you heard? Riley is running away."

I couldn't even speak. Riley wasn't a girl who ran away. Riley was *happy*! Why was everything falling apart?

"Joy, if we hurry, we can still stop her," Sadness said.

Yes, she was right. We had to move. We had to get to another island, then get to Headquarters from there. But what islands were left? I looked around desperately until I saw it.

"Family Island," I said. "Let's go!"

We ran as fast as we could toward Family Island, but it was already starting to shake and crumble.

"No!" I moaned. "That's our only way back!"

Then I saw one of the shelves in Long Term break, exposing a recall tube! That would take us directly back to Headquarters. We all ran toward it. Family Island was falling apart around us, so we had no time. I entered the recall tube, holding my satchel of core memories tight. Sadness crammed herself into the tube right beside me, but it was too tight a squeeze. She pushed up against the core memories, and when I peeked into the bag, I saw them start to turn blue!

"Whoa, whoa!" I snapped. "Sadness, stop! You are hurting Riley!"

I pulled out one of the core memories to show Sadness how it was changing, and she stepped back, stunned.

"If you get in here, these core memories will get sad," I said.

I looked at Sadness, then at the memories, and then at Family Island, which was nearly gone. For a moment I was frozen—I didn't know what to do! Then I thought about Riley, and I knew there was only one choice.

"I'm sorry. Riley needs to be happy," I told Sadness. I placed the memory sphere back in the satchel, sealed it tight, and then pulled the recall tube closed. I began to ride up the tube . . . alone.

Unfortunately, the tube wasn't strong enough to handle the earthquake of Family Island falling to shreds. It broke apart and I fell out just as the ground below the tubes gave way and collapsed. Sadness panicked and leaped back from the new crevasse. Bing Bong leaped forward and reached out to me. But he ended up falling, too.

I don't know how long I dropped. It seemed like forever. Then I landed with a thud. When I opened my eyes, I saw only dim light from up above, and more memory spheres than I'd ever seen in one place. They seemed not as bright as most memory spheres, but maybe I was just getting used to the darkness. Panic coursed through me as I realized I'd dropped the satchel of core memories, but then I saw them a few feet away and quickly slung the bag over my shoulder.

I looked up. What I saw almost knocked all hope out of me. I was so deep in the Memory Dump, I could barely see the light from above.

Driven By Emotions

"No, no, no, no!" I cried. I tried to race up a hill of memories, but it was too short to reach the top and too steep to climb. I only slid back down. I couldn't stop trying, though. Again and again I clawed my way up, but I never got any higher, never any closer to that light up above.

"Joy?" a voice called. "Joy."

It was Bing Bong. I'd forgotten he had fallen down there with me.

"Joy, don't you get it? We're stuck down here. We're forgotten," said Bing Bong.

Forgotten?

No, that couldn't be right.

I looked down at the memories at my feet. They *had* seemed dimmer than usual, but . . .

Suddenly, one faded away to nothingness.

Gone.

Forgotten.

I had failed for the first time ever, and my insides were churning around like crazy. Then I saw the blue core memory lying on the ground. It was the memory of Riley crying in front of her class. I picked it up and watched tears pour down Riley's cheeks. I fell to my knees and began to cry. My heart was broken.

There were so many faded memories around me. Most of them were moments so tiny I hadn't even thought of them in ages. I watched two-year-old Riley sticking her tongue out while she was coloring.

"I just wanted Riley to be happy," I told Bing Bong, "and now . . ."

I sobbed. I don't think I'd ever cried before. Maybe a sniffle or two when Riley was hurt, but this was different. It was like my whole body was heaving up and pouring out through my tears. Bing Bong sat there next to me and rubbed my back a little, but the tears just kept coming until I didn't have any more. When I was done, I felt like a wrung-out washcloth.

I looked around. Faded memories kept disappearing. Every second, more bits of Riley's past went away. It was too awful to watch. I pulled out my favorite memory from the satchel—the one at the twisty tree. I started to watch it, but a last tear fell onto the sphere. When I wiped it away, the color of the memory changed from gold . . . to blue.

That was strange. That had never happened before. Had Sadness done something to this memory?

The image on the screen wasn't familiar anymore. Riley wasn't with the whole team; she was sitting in the branch of the twisty tree with Mom and Dad, and she looked . . . sad.

I must have rewound the memory when I wiped away the tear. I rewound it further now. Riley was all alone, sitting in the tree and crying . . . sobbing, just like I had been a second ago.

I remembered what Sadness had said about that memory: that Riley had missed the winning shot in the game and felt so awful she wanted to quit. Then Mom and Dad came to talk to her— because of Sadness! They came to talk to Riley because of Sadness. My entire favorite happy memory . . . it wouldn't have happened if Sadness hadn't gotten Mom, Dad, and the team to comfort

Riley—the same way Sadness had comforted Bing Bong in Imagination Land.

Riley *needed* Sadness. The same way she needed me. In fact, maybe Riley's Joy was even more joyful because she also had Sadness in her life.

It was crazy enough to make my head want to explode, but all of a sudden, I knew for a fact that it was true. I had to find Sadness and bring her back to Headquarters right away!

"Come on, Bing Bong!" I shouted, leaping to my feet. "We have to get back up there!"

"Joy," he said sadly, "we're stuck down here. We might as well be on another planet."

Another planet. Yes! Another planet! Bing Bong had wanted to take Riley to the moon in his rocket . . . a rocket that was already thrown into the dump and ran on song power! I started singing as loud as I could. It took a while, but then we heard the rocket beeping back at us! We ran to the sound and dug down through fading memories until we found it. Then we dragged it to the perfect spot, a place in the dump with two giant hills of memories:

one we could ride down to gain speed, and one we could zoom up again. If we got the rocket moving quickly enough, we could soar off the top of the second hill and shoot all the way back up to the Long Term Memory cliffs!

We pulled the rocket to the top of the first hill and climbed in. As we rolled down, Bing Bong and I both sang his song. The rocket gained power with each word. It roared to life, picking up speed as it raced down one hill and up the other. It was moving so quickly at the top of the second hill that it soared into the air . . .

. . . and crashed to the ground long before it got anywhere near the cliff's edge.

I couldn't give up, though. Bing Bong and I dragged the rocket all the way back to the first hill. We sang even louder, even stronger, and the rocket felt more powerful under our bodies. I just knew this time we'd make it out.

Except we didn't. We crashed again. We needed something more—a way to get more power—but I didn't know what to do.

"Come on, Joy, one more time," Bing Bong said. "I've got a feeling about this one."

So we tried again. We did things a little differently this time. Bing Bong found the steepest memory hill, and we dragged the rocket all the way to its tip-top. We both climbed into the rocket and sang Bing Bong's song, and when the rocket roared to life, we sang even *louder*. We whipped down the first hill and zoomed up the second one. Suddenly, it felt like we shot forward with an extra boost of energy. The rocket flew off the top of that second hill, soared into the air . . .

. . . and made the jump! The rocket flew all the way out of the dump and landed on the cliff's edge. Bing Bong and I were saved!

"Woo-hoo!" I cheered. "Bing Bong, we did it! We—"

But then I turned around and realized Bing Bong was gone.

"Bing Bong?" I called. "Bing Bong!"

I heard laughter. I looked down into the dump. He was there. Bing Bong. He was dancing and smiling and happier than I'd ever seen him.

"Ya-ha-ha!" he cheered. "You made it! Go! Go save Riley! Take her to the moon for me, okay?"

He waved good-bye . . . then disappeared. Riley's imaginary friend was gone forever.

"I'll try, Bing Bong. I promise," I said.

Suddenly, I understood. That's why the rocket had been so fast on the second hill. Bing Bong had jumped off. He'd sacrificed himself for me. For Riley.

It was the most loving thing I'd ever seen anyone do.

I wanted to take a moment to sit there and think about him, but the world around me started to rumble, and I knew I didn't have time. I had to get back to Headquarters, and first I needed to find Sadness. But where? I darted back into the Long Term Memory shelves and noticed all the memories on the bottom shelves were blue—as though someone very sad had been running her hands over them as she walked.

"Sadness!" I called, and took off running,

following the blue path. Soon I found her, far up ahead, and I knew she'd run to me when I called her, and we could get to Headquarters right away. "Sadness! Sadness!"

Sadness turned and saw me, but instead of running toward me, she ran away.

"Sadness!" I cried.

"Just let me go," she said. "Riley's better off without me."

"Come back!" I wailed, but Sadness was still running, and she had a huge head start. I chased her all the way through Long Term Memory and into Imagination Land. She lost me in the French Fry Forest, then I found her again in Cloud City but she grabbed a cloud and soared too far overhead for me to catch her. Soon she was floating above the remnants of Family Island, which at this point was little more than some debris and the trampoline that used to support the whole structure.

The trampoline . . .

I suddenly had the craziest idea ever in the history of crazy ideas. I ran to the Imaginary

Boyfriend Generator I'd seen earlier when Bing Bong had taken Sadness and me on the Imagination Land tour. The boyfriend was still moping next to it, peeling petals off a flower.

"You!" I said. "Did you mean what you said before?"

"I would die for Riley!" he moaned. "I would die for Riley. I would die—"

"Yeah, yeah." I shushed him. "Time to prove it."

I scooped the imaginary boyfriend into my bottomless satchel, then started up the generator to turn more and more of them out. As they came down the conveyer belt, I caught each one in my satchel. Then I ran along the cliff's edge toward Friendship Island. Once I had Sadness in sight, I aligned myself with her and poured out all the imaginary boyfriends from the satchel. They quickly stacked up below me—standing on each other's shoulders—until they formed a very wobbly tower. And I was at the very top!

"Whoa!" I yelled. The tower was so unsteady I nearly fell!

"This is crazy, this is crazy . . ." I muttered to myself. "No, no, no! Joy! Be positive!"

I made the mistake of looking down again.

"I am positive that this is crazy!" I said.

I looked out at the trampoline on Family Island, then at Sadness floating just past it, and then at Headquarters high above her. If I just timed everything right . . .

"NOW!" I yelled.

All the imaginary boyfriends leaned forward, launching me onto the Family Island trampoline. I bounced off it, then zoomed into the air at the perfect trajectory to catch Sadness.

"Joy?" she said, surprised.

"Hang on!" I cried, because we weren't done yet. We were still soaring up, up, up . . . until we *smacked* into the window of Headquarters.

We quickly slid *down* the window and, at the last second, grabbed the window ledge. I then managed to reach up and bang on the window until I saw Fear, Anger, and Disgust rush over. They were all wide-eyed with shock.

That was when I realized a little error in my plan. The windows of Headquarters don't open! How were they going to let us in?

I honestly have no idea how it happened but, suddenly, a giant circular hole appeared in the window, big enough for Sadness and me to climb through.

"Thank goodness you're back!" Fear cried.

I looked past him and saw what was happening with Riley on the view screen.

She was on a bus, all by herself. Running away. And I knew I couldn't stop her on my own.

"Sadness," I said, "it's up to you."

"Me?" she asked. "I can't, Joy."

But I knew she could. I led her to the console. It was her turn to drive. She held her hand over the controls and removed the idea bulb. Riley's face changed. It went from pinched and angry to open and sad. Her eyes welled. And after a minute, she jumped up and told the bus driver to stop the bus because she wanted to get off. The bus driver listened, and Riley ran all the way home.

Mom and Dad had been so worried they didn't know whether to hug Riley or scream at her when she got there, but I knew what to do. I handed Sadness all of Riley's core memories, the ones I'd been protecting all this time. When Sadness touched them, they turned completely blue. And as she placed each memory in the projector, Riley remembered each one of them. She recalled baking cookies with Mom and Dad when she was little. She remembered running around the living room with her underpants on her head, and Dad chasing after her with a towel. She remembered the time when she scored her first hockey goal, and when she used to skate on the frozen lake with Mom and Dad.

Riley remembered all of these moments and began to cry.

"I know you don't want me to," she sobbed, "but I miss home. I miss Minnesota. You need me to be happy, but I want my old friends back, and my hockey team. I wanna go home. Please don't be mad."

They weren't. Mom and Dad saw how sad she was and they just comforted her. They said they missed home, too. And even though all three of them were really sad, they were sad together. And that was kind of . . . joyful.

As Riley, Mom, and Dad all hugged, I gave Sadness her blue core memory which I had retrieved from the Memory Dump. Sadness smiled at me and took my hand. She led me over to the console and placed my hand next to hers, so we could drive together.

PING!

I knew that wonderful sound. A new core memory was being created! And it was like no other memory we had seen before. Instead of being a single color, this core memory was blue and gold, all swirled together. The other Emotions and I stared in awe as the new core memory sphere rolled into Headquarters and settled in the core memory holder. Then a lightline emerged from the back of Headquarters into the Mind World, generating a brand-new Family Island! It was far bigger and even more beautiful than the original one.

I rested my head on Sadness, and we both smiled. Riley was going to be just fine now. And so were we.

So, you know, that was a little while ago, and since then things have changed a lot in ol' Headquarters. The core memories? They're not all golden yellow anymore. Each one is made of swirls of all of our colors. And that's had a huge impact on the new Islands of Personality. They've all grown back now, and they're better than ever! Friendship Island has expanded, and recently opened a Friendly Argument section, which Anger loves. Sadness has a particular fondness for Tragic Vampire Romance Island. Boy Band Island . . . we're kind of hoping that one's just a phase, but honestly, I'm thrilled with all of it. And we even have a new, expanded console with so many kinds of buttons and levers and gadgets. The best thing about it is that it has space for all five of us to drive together at the same time.

Turns out we make an amazing team.

Everything is pretty fantastic. And I feel like we really have it all together now, just like Riley. Our girl is amazing. She has great new friends, a great new house . . . things couldn't be better. After all, Riley's twelve now. What could happen?

Disgust

Ugh, okay, I guess I'm supposed to tell you about the big move to San Francisco and how Joy, Sadness, Anger, Fear, and I ended up working together at one big console (a console that gives us nowhere near enough personal space, if you ask me). Fine. Whatever. Here goes.

So the whole thing started when Riley was a baby. That's when I showed up, and seriously, I'm not sure how the girl got along without me. From what I hear, they were feeding Riley mysterious mushy green stuff before I hit the scene, and that is *not* acceptable. I got there around the time of solid food, and believe me, if it wasn't brightly colored or shaped like a dinosaur, there was no

Driven By Emotions

way I was letting Riley eat it. Broccoli for example? Immediate spit-out.

So life was what it was and it all worked out fine for Riley, because I was so ready to step in and save her from anything disgusting, including out-of-fashion clothes and bad music. Not on my watch.

Then came the news that we were moving from Minnesota to San Francisco.

Are you kidding me?

First of all, we took the trip in a station wagon. *No one* looks cool in a station wagon. Why couldn't Mom and Dad have rented an awesome convertible for the trip? And to make matters worse, we were *in* that station wagon for just this side of forever. Do you have any idea how many smells three people generate when they're in a small space for that long? Gross! Then we finally got to San Francisco . . . um . . . have you ever seen that place? All those murals on the walls, like anyone wants to see bad public art. I swear, some of the buildings looked like they were made of garbage, and the hills . . . I can't with the hills. I just can't.

So we got to the city, and then we found Riley's new house, which was basically an abomination of dirt and grime stuck together with termite saliva. That was the outside. It smelled like something died on the inside. You know why? Because something did. We saw a *dead mouse*. Not acceptable. The only thing that would have made it even remotely okay was a full sanitizing followed by a major decorating plan that involved every one of Riley's cutest possessions, but you know what? The moving van with all those possessions had gone missing. Horrifying, and horrifying again. We were left with no barrier between us and the cramped prison cell that was now Riley's room.

Joy thought we'd feel better if we had a great lunch, and she suggested a pizza place we saw on the way into town. I'm all for pizza. It's totally on my acceptable list, especially if it has cheese that's gooey enough to stretch, but not so gooey it breaks off and dangles down Riley's chin until it looks like she's spitting it up. But this San Francisco pizza place? It put *broccoli* on the pizza! That's not food, it's torture! And it was the only option they had! I wasn't sure what to do first: grab my barf bag or call the health inspector and let him know the place was shoving out poison.

The clear verdict? Moving to San Francisco was a horrible disaster and the worst decision Mom and Dad had ever made. Fear, Anger, and I were beyond upset, but then Joy showed us some hysterical memories, and that was pretty fun. If I could have just watched those, I would have forgotten all about the Broccoli Pizza Monster, and everything would've been fine.

But then something weird happened. We were all looking at a funny memory when, suddenly, it turned blue and sad. Doesn't make sense, right? So we turned around and saw Sadness touching the memory. I was completely disgusted. I mean, the memory was of Dad forgetting to put the emergency brakes on the station wagon and letting it roll into a dinosaur tail. That's brilliant stuff! But Sadness had wrecked it!

"Good going, Sadness," I said. "Now when Riley

thinks of that moment with Dad, she's gonna feel sad. Bravo."

Sadness had never done much around Headquarters before. Seriously, she was like this blue lump. And not only did she leave puddles of tears on the ground, she was starting to change happy memories to sad ones! Gross. I totally got it when Joy told Sadness to keep her paws *off* the memories.

At the same time, if Sadness was freaking out, I totally got *that*, too. I didn't like anything about this move, either. And that night, instead of sleeping in her own beautiful room back in Minnesota, Riley was in a sleeping bag on the floor of her new tiny, dust-covered, mouse-apocalypse room. Ugh! I was over it. Totally over it. Then Mom came in to kiss Riley good night, and she was all, "Thanks, Riley, for being so happy when our whole life rots and we made this hideous decision to move to this place of doom." I might be paraphrasing. Point is, she was pretty cool about Riley's attitude in the face of all this change and upheaval, so I felt like Joy knew what she was doing with her whole stay-happy-no-matter-what deal.

I went to bed after that. Any time I could spend not awake in San Fran-*sick*-o was time well spent. Plus I needed the rest. The next day was the first day of school, which is basically a giant experiment in social horror. I had to get Riley completely prepared with the right outfit and the right things to say if she was going to get in with the cool kids and have any kind of life whatsoever.

The next morning, we all rallied in Headquarters, and Joy gave us jobs.

"Disgust," she said, "make sure Riley stands out today . . . but also blends in."

Oh, please. Like I wasn't already on that like algae on an unclean pool.

"When I'm through," I said, "Riley will look so good the other kids will look at their own outfits and barf."

I *totally* delivered. Riley had a super-cute outfit, a cool backpack with a funky pattern, and great styled hair that bounced from side to side as she walked. Riley walked into the school with confidence and just enough swagger to *intrigue* other kids, not turn them off. She had a smile that said "I'm fun" as opposed to "I'm desperate." She was ready.

"Okay, we've got a group of cool girls at two o'clock," I said as I watched Riley's progress on the big screen.

"How do you know?" Joy asked.

"Double ears pierced, infinity scarf . . ." Please. It was so obvious. Then they turned and looked at us, and one of them was wearing eye shadow. "Yeah," I told Joy, "we want to be friends with them."

Then Joy said she wanted to go talk with them! And I was like, "Are you kidding? We're not *talking* to them. We want them to like us!"

Riley had a shot at it, too. She was playing it totally cool. Even when the ridiculous teacher put her through the torture of talking about herself in front of the entire class—whatever—Joy had it under control. She recalled a memory of Riley and her parents skating together. Then Riley started talking about Minnesota, and playing hockey. It scored major cool-girl points, I could tell.

Then, out of nowhere, she got all sniffly and sad.

"We go out on the lake almost every weekend. Or we did," Riley said, "'until I moved away."

Our view screen in Headquarters turned completely blue. We all spun around, and *Sadness* had her hands on the memory sphere. Like, what was she thinking?! You couldn't make Riley *sad* at a pivotal moment like this! She was practically on stage, auditioning to be part of the social hierarchy, and thanks to Sadness, she was now totally blowing it. Joy frantically pushed buttons on the console to remove the sphere from the projector, but it wouldn't budge! And Riley was falling apart.

"We used to play tag and stuff . . ." she sniffed.

Tag?! You don't talk about a baby game to your new classmates! I scanned the room around Riley. It was bad.

"Cool kids whispering at three o'clock," I said.

Somebody had to do something. Joy, Fear,

Anger, and I tried to pull the stuck memory from the projector, but it wouldn't budge!

Riley, meanwhile? Full-on sobfest. *Very bad*. It was a moment that everyone watching would still be talking about at their twenty-year high school reunion. "Remember that lame kid who sobbed in front of us on her first day of school?"

Yeah, that's where we were headed. And to cap it off, Sadness was now driving the console. Joy finally yanked the stuck memory out of the projector and pulled Sadness off the console. That's when it happened. Oh, yeah. We all saw it roll into Headquarters.

"It's a core memory!" Fear wailed.

"But it's *blue*!" I sneered. I mean, seriously, since when does Riley have blue core memories? She doesn't. They're all yellow. Blue doesn't even go with the color scheme in the core memory holder. Clearly Joy agreed with me, because she ran to the core memory holder and popped it up, causing the sphere to hit the edge and roll back.

Then she grabbed the blue core memory and

pushed a button to lower the vacuum tube that sends all the memories down to Long Term. She was going to get rid of it! But then Sadness tried to grab it back from her. It got so crazy between them that they—and you're not going to believe this—bumped the core memory holder and *the five core memories spilled out.*

It was totally freaky to see them rolling around on the floor. I screamed, and not much outside a bloody hangnail makes me scream. Then *all* of Riley's Islands of Personality went dark. And that was a huge problem. The islands make Riley *Riley.* If they were down, who would she become? It was true horror movie material. And since horror movies are generally gross, I really didn't like where things seemed to be heading.

I didn't know what to do. I watched as Joy scrambled to gather the five yellow core memories. Sadness grabbed the new blue one and tried to put it into the core memory holder, but Joy lunged at her! As they began pushing each other back and forth, they got super close to the vacuum tube . . .

And then they both got sucked inside!

For a moment, I thought they'd get stuck and plug it up, but they didn't. They disappeared completely. Who knew where they'd end up . . . somewhere deep in the Mind World.

Fear, Anger, and I just stood there for a minute, watching the spot where they'd left.

"What are we supposed to do now?" Anger finally roared. "They left us here with a whole ruined school day to handle!"

"I know what to do!" Fear cried. "Let's curl up in the fetal position and hide!"

That's what he did. Curled up in a ball and shut his eyes, because I guess he figured if he couldn't see us, we couldn't see him. Whatever.

"You're not hiding, Fear," I said. "Come on, we have to take the controls until Joy comes back."

"*Will* she come back?" Fear asked. "*WILL* she?!"

I rolled my eyes. "Of course she will. Where else would she go?"

And seriously, in the meantime, we needed to do something about Riley. After a little maneuvering, we got her sitting back at her desk and had her disappear in a book. It was a textbook, which wasn't ideal. I'd rather she'd had her nose in some super-hip postapocalyptic novel, ideally one that was made into a movie, but we used what we had.

Honestly, we didn't have a lot of time to take stock and think until Riley was having dinner. Up until then we were just working overtime to get her through the school day. Anger had her snap at a bunch of kids who kept tapping their pencils on the desk, Fear got her all freaked out when she found cobwebs in her locker, and don't even get me started on how I handled the cafeteria lunch at Riley's new school. Tortilla soup? A tortilla is a flat slice of not-bread. How do you make it into a soup? Even if you pounded it up and pulverized it into a soup, you wouldn't get cheese and red goo out of it. What is the red goo, anyway? Thank goodness I'm here to ask these questions.

Then came dinnertime. Joy and Sadness still weren't back, so it was just me, Fear, and Anger in a Headquarters that felt completely bleak with no core memories. Not a pleasant work environment, and I made sure Anger and Fear knew I was working under duress in less than ideal conditions.

Fear had a brilliant idea, and by brilliant, I mean absurd. He said all we had to do until Joy got back was to be just like her. "Just do what Joy would do," he said.

"Great idea," I muttered. "How are WE supposed to be happy?"

Before we could figure that out, Mom started yammering about a new hockey team and tryouts tomorrow. She needed a response. Anger looked at me, like I would know what to do.

"What do we do?" I asked.

"You pretend to be Joy," said Fear.

Ugh. Gag me. But Fear pushed me to the console, so I had no choice. "Fine," I said. "Whatever." I took the controls, and when Mom started getting giggly about hockey again—like we'd even care about hockey after the day we'd had—I had Riley roll her eyes and say, "Oh, yeah, that sounds fantastic." Then Fear got all up in my grill because I didn't sound like Joy, but for real—I'm *not* Joy.

I thought that would be it, but Mom didn't give up. She thought something was wrong with Riley—which, hello, it totally was, but Mom would never understand. She started asking lots of questions and looking for deep, meaningful answers. I was over it, so I turned the controls to Fear. Let him be Joy and see how it worked for *him*.

In a word? It didn't. Mom asked how school was and Fear had Riley basically curl up in a ball and hide.

"It was fine, I guess. I don't know," she said.

Pretty much *just* like Joy. Not. So then Anger tried to be Joy. That caused a full-on meltdown that got Riley sent to her room without dessert. Complete disaster. Then, a little later that night, Dad came into her room to try to make things better. He started acting silly and goofy, which normally would start up Goofball Island, but Goofball Island was dark. And you know what happens when you start up a broken island?

Of course you don't. I didn't either. Turns out it

crumbles and falls to pieces. We saw it all happen from Headquarters. So that left Riley's mind filled with what? Rubble. Rubble in her head. How gross is that? *Clearly* we needed Joy back. She'd know how to de-rubble-ify the place. Without her, we were just winging it, and I don't do the improv thing.

Still, we had to try to keep things together. So that night, when Riley's best friend from home, Meg, called Riley on her laptop, Fear, Anger, and I were ready at the console. I figured it would be easy girl stuff, nothing too difficult. I mean, Riley and Meg had known each other forever. We could handle a simple conversation.

But then you know what Meg said? Riley asked about the hockey play-offs because she and Meg had been on the same team, and Meg was all, "Oh, we've got this new girl on the team. She's so cool."

She was saying that to us for real? How gross is that? Just throw your new BFF in our face, am I right? Anger was furious. Fear was freaking out. I was nauseated, but I tried to keep it under control because I could see out the window that

Friendship Island was having a minor earthquake over the conversation and was in major danger of crumbling.

No use. Meg got Anger too furious. I saw it coming the minute Meg said, "We can pass the puck to each other without even looking. It's like mind reading."

"You like to read minds, Meg?" Anger roared. "I got something for you to read, right here!"

"Hey, hey, no!" I yelled. "What are you doing?"

Anger had Riley yell and slam her computer shut . . . and we lost Friendship Island. More mind rubble.

The next day we had school again. Seriously? Who came up with the whole school-five-days-a-week thing? I mean, it's overkill. Riley already needed a weekend to decompress. Instead, she had to trudge through this sea of judging kids. Each one of them stopped to point and gawk at the new kid who cried in class.

Yeah, okay, maybe they didn't *actually* stop and point, but mentally they did. I could see it in their eyes. Especially the cool girls' eyes. They had no clue how awesome Riley really was, and they were never going to give us a chance to prove it. Not anymore.

I couldn't let Riley deal with that nonsense. I made sure she brought a book along to school. A good book—some giant intimidating-looking thing Mom had brought from home in the station wagon. I had Riley pull it out before each class and act like she was *way* too engrossed to care that no one wanted to talk to her. It worked for lunch, too. She sat on a bench all by herself and kept her nose in that book while she picked at the cafeteria slop. That way everyone knew she was way too cool to care what a bunch of kids thought about her.

The book thing worked for school, but after school we had to deal with something more challenging: those hockey tryouts Mom had been talking about the night before. Tryouts might have been fine if Riley had her core memories and Hockey Island was still running, but she didn't and it wasn't. It was dark. So Fear, Anger, and I knew what would happen if Riley attempted to play hockey. It was going to get real ugly, real quick.

When we arrived at the hockey rink, I quickly looked around. I didn't see any of the cool kids there. At least that was a relief. I did *not* want them to see what was about to happen to Riley.

"Good luck, sweetie!" Mom cheered as Riley took the ice.

"Luck isn't going to help us now," I told Anger and Fear. "If she tries to use Hockey Island, it's going down."

That's how it seemed to work. If Riley tried to activate an island without the core memory to power it, the whole island would crumble.

But Fear had a solution. He had recalled every hockey memory he could think of to take the place of the core memory. Yep, he had us knee-deep in memory spheres.

"One of these has got to work in place of the core memory," Fear said.

Yeah. Like he knew. But, hey, we had to try. We started pumping hockey memories into the core memory holder. Fear ran to the window to check on Hockey Island. Even I could see it was lighting up. Not much, but a little.

"Ha-ha!" Fear cheered. "We did it! It's working—"

BOOM! The core memory holder flat-out rejected one of the memory spheres; blew it out like a bullet and nailed Anger right in the stomach.

I laughed. Just for a second. You totally would have, too—little, red Anger getting whopped like that. But then he roared back to the console and he was—shocker—furious. He took the controls and had Riley play without even thinking, just slapping the puck around and . . . I'm not even going to pretend I know anything about hockey, but whatever Riley was doing wasn't hockey. It was ugly, and soon she stormed off the rink and tore off her skates. Mom tried to calm her down and tell her everything was going to be okay, which just proved she knew *nothing* about what was going on in Riley's head.

"Stop saying everything will be all right!" Riley roared, and then stomped out of the building.

You can guess what happened to Hockey Island, right? Rubble.

By that night, I couldn't even deal anymore. "On a scale of one to ten," I said, "I give this day an F."

"Well, why don't we quit standing around and do something?" Anger asked.

"Like what, genius?" I pressed him.

"Like quitting," Fear said. "That's what I'm doing."

For real. He was. He had a recall tube coming down and he was going to zip away to who-knows-where like Joy and Sadness. But of course, this was Fear. He couldn't even quit correctly. He got sucked halfway into the tube, got stuck, and practically smeared his face off on the tube.

Can you believe I have to live with these two? Me neither.

"Emotions can't quit, genius," I said.

"Wait a minute," Anger said. "Wait a minute!" He started rummaging through Riley's idea bulbs, then held one up like it was something special.

"What is it?" Fear asked.

"Oh, nothing . . . just the best idea ever," Anger said.

"What?" I asked.

"All the good core memories were made in Minnesota," Anger said. "Ergo, we go back to Minnesota and make more. Ta-da!"

"Wait, wait, wait," said Fear. "You're saying . . . we run away?"

"Well, I wouldn't call it that. I'd call it the Happy Core Memory Development Program."

It still sounded majorly gross to me. If I'm traveling, I want to travel in comfort. Running away would *not* equal comfort. It would equal cheap food and smelly buses.

Of course, our new home wasn't much better. And Anger was right, we'd had it pretty good in Minnesota.

Fear suggested we sleep on it. I was cool with that. Beauty sleep always helped. This time, though, I didn't sleep well at all. And when I woke up, Fear was quaking under the console. "What is going on?" I asked.

"We were at school," he blabbered, "and we were naked, and there was a dog, and his back half was chasing him . . . and then we saw Bing Bong."

"You idiot!" Anger screamed. "It was a *dream*! This is ridiculous, and we can't even get a good night's sleep anymore. Time to take action." He grabbed the idea bulb he'd had earlier—the one about running away. "Stupid Mom and Dad," he grumbled. "If they hadn't moved us, none of this would've happened." He moved the idea to the console, where he could plug it in and make it an official live idea in Riley's mind. "Who's with me?" Anger asked.

I thought about it for a moment. Running away was a big deal. But honestly, things couldn't get any worse.

"Yeah," I said. "Let's do it."

Anger plugged the idea into the console, and Riley sat up in bed, inspired. She pulled out her laptop.

"So how're we gonna get to Minnesota from here?" I asked.

"Well, why don't we go to the elephant lot and rent an elephant?" Anger railed.

Seriously, the sarcasm I have to deal with. It's like a joke.

"What do you think?" Anger continued. "We're taking the bus!"

The smelly, crowded bus. Private jet would be more my speed, but I guess that wasn't so much an option. Honestly, I didn't even know if a bus was an option. "A ticket costs money," I noted. "How do we get money?"

"Mom's purse," Anger said.

"You wouldn't!" I gasped.

"Oh, but I would," Anger assured me. "Where was Mom's purse when we saw it last?"

I'd never really thought of Riley as a thief—thieves are pretty disgusting—but Anger had a point. Mom and Dad got us into this mess, so it made sense they should pay to get us out.

Anger had the controls, and he led Riley downstairs. Mom was on the phone, and the purse was on the table. It was seriously simple to pull open the purse, slip out a credit card, and run back upstairs. I was pretty impressed. Oh, sure, Honesty Island crumbled to dust the minute we did it, but at this point, what was one less island?

The next morning, instead of loading books in her backpack, Riley packed some clothes. We were serious about running away now, and that had Family Island pretty shaky, but Mom and Dad were kind of getting what they deserved on that score. I mean, really, weren't they the ones who'd hurt Family Island by moving us away? Yeah, I thought so, too. Sure, Mom and Dad acted all nice and said they'd see us after school. But that only proved how clueless they were! How could they be so cheery? Didn't they know how much trouble they'd caused by changing everything on us?

Riley didn't go to school that day. After she packed her backpack (I made sure she had a good selection of outfits—after all, she was going to have to get by with very little for a while), she walked out the front door without saying a single word to Mom and Dad. She then headed for the bus station. The bus wasn't scheduled to leave until much later in the afternoon, so we had some time to kill.

Fear was paranoid that we'd get lost once we got to Minnesota, so he steered Riley into the public library to borrow some maps. And while she was there, she decided to flip through books about runaway kids. Again, one of Fear's brilliant ideas. He wanted to know what was in store for us, and ended up giving himself an anxiety attack.

As freaky as those books were, they didn't deter Riley from carrying out our plan. She put the books back on the shelf and left the library. Thank goodness. Public places are gross—totally full of germs. I mean, who knows how many people could have picked their noses and wiped their boogers on those chairs and shelves. Blech!

So we resumed our walk to the bus station. It was a grueling, unforgiving, relentless walk. If I hadn't been convinced before that we needed to get as far away from San Francisco as possible, the walk did it. With all those hills, it was a plod. And then we went through this dirty park. I must have seen bird poop on every bench. And, I don't know, call me crazy, but back in Minnesota, when you walked by someone, they said hi. They just did, whether or not they knew you. Here? No one. Yeah, yeah, I know Riley had her head down like she didn't want to talk to anyone, but still—how about some manners, San Francisco?

Worst part? The last few blocks before the station smelled like feet and sewage. Nothing in Minnesota smelled like feet and sewage. We'd be *soooo* much happier back there.

Mom called as we approached the bus station, but we were *not* going to answer and deal with that nonsense. Riley kept her head down and her nose as closed as possible, and we finally made it to the bus station . . . which, of course, smelled like pee. I totally didn't get it—did people seriously think the corners of the building were an okay place to do their business? What were they, dogs marking their territory?

Riley was in line for tickets when Mom called again. She'd called fifteen times already.

DISGUST

Fear, Anger, and I heard a horrible sound. It hurt my ears—it was all rumbly and screechy and . . . it was the sound of Family Island collapsing.

"We're losing the last island!" I screamed.

"This is madness! She shouldn't run away!" Anger yelled.

"Let's get that idea out of her head," I said.

We tried. We seriously tried hard-core. But the idea wouldn't budge from the console. It wouldn't unscrew. Worse, it got fire-hot so we couldn't even touch it! "Now what?" I asked.

Then things got weird.

All the controls started shutting down. This nasty black yuckiness spread over the console. None of us had ever seen anything like it.

"Get that idea out of there!" I screamed.

Anger tried to slam a chair down on the console, but it just bounced off. Fear tried prying the idea out with a crowbar, but the bar just popped out and smacked him in the face . . . which would have been funny at any other time, but now I was way too freaked out to laugh at his expense.

"How do we stop it?" Fear wailed.

I had an idea. "Make her feel scared! She might change her mind!"

"Yes!" Fear cried. "Brilliant!"

"I know it's brilliant," I snapped. "Do it!"

Fear tried. He pushed every button.

"Guys," he said, and there was something in his voice I'd never heard before. A fear deeper than anything he'd ever shared. "We can't make Riley feel anything."

"What have we done?" Anger asked.

I wondered the same thing. We'd messed up big-time, and now Riley was hunched on a bus, running away from the people who loved her.

"That's it," Anger said. "It's over. There's nothing more to do."

At that moment, I heard banging on the back window. I ran over to investigate.

"It's Joy!" I shouted.

She and Sadness were hanging on to the outside of the window! Who knows how they got there, but they wanted in. Just one problem . . .

none of the windows in Headquarters opened.

"Stand back!" Anger roared. He threw a chair at the window, but it still wouldn't open. These guys and their throwing things—do they really think it's an effective way to get things done?

"Brilliant," I chided him.

"Well, what would you do, if you're so smart!?" he challenged me.

You *don't* want to challenge me. Watching him smolder, the little flames flickering on the top of his red, square body, I knew *exactly* what to do.

"I'd tell you, but you're too dumb to understand," I said.

"WHAT?" he spat.

"Of course your tiny brain is confused. Guess I'll have to dumb it down to your level. Sorry I don't speak 'moron' as well as you, but let me try . . ."

I made the dumbest face I possibly could. "Duuuuuhhhhh."

That put him over the edge. His head became a blowtorch of flames as he screamed, so I picked him up and used his head to cut a hole in the glass.

Bingo—Joy and Sadness were in. And, yes, I am brilliant. Thank you.

It was good timing, too, because we all saw what was going down on the view screen in Headquarters. The bus was driving away with Riley on it. I was sure Joy would start driving the console and make everything all right. But Joy did no such thing.

"Sadness," she said, "it's up to you."

And Sadness . . . *Sadness*, of all the Emotions, took the console. She drove, and Riley's face got all misty and, well . . . sad. A second later, Riley jumped up and told the bus driver to stop so she could get off. Riley went home and poured her heart out to her worried parents, and, I've got to say, Mom and Dad did okay. They didn't do any crazy parent stuff like yell for no reason. They let Riley talk and they cried and hugged, and I wasn't even grossed out when their faces got puffy from the tears.

That was a bunch of months ago, and now things are different for all of us Emotions. Even Headquarters is different. The core memories are a mix of different colors now—yellow, blue, red, purple, and even a little green for some healthy disgust. I thought the colors wouldn't blend well, but it totally works. And Joy isn't so much in charge anymore. We all drive together on a brand-new, upgraded console. Yeah, sure, it's great, but as I said earlier, driving together means very little personal space. And I need my personal space.

Big picture, though? Things are good. And Riley's killing it at school. Her friends are massively cool—way cooler than the cool kids I thought she wanted to hang with at first. Plus the house is super cute now with all of Riley's stuff in it. I've made sure she has the right posters on the walls. We even found a pizza place that serves the real deal—nothing green on it whatsoever.

And can you believe Riley's twelve now? Twelve and fabulous! It'll be smooth sailing from here. Sure, there are a few things on the new console that we don't understand yet, like a little warning light labeled PUBERTY. Joy doesn't think it's important, though. And, honestly, I've taken care of the hard stuff already. Riley is totally set for an awesome life with great friends, awesome parents, a way-cool fashion sense, and impeccable taste in just about everything . . . thanks to *moi!*

Fear

Oh, man. It's my turn to tell you our story . . . the story about moving to San Francisco and how it all got crazy, and Riley was nearly kidnapped and whisked away forever to end up living in a sewer and begging for change on the street . . .

Okay, I'm running away with myself. I do that sometimes. Sorry. I just get so nervous when I think about what could have happened and how bad it could have been . . . but again, getting ahead of the story.

I'll start from the start. Riley's start. Well, I wasn't there for the *very* start. I came a little later, when Riley was a toddler. You wouldn't believe the disasters she almost got into every day. I was working overtime, I promise you that. She'd just run with complete abandon—if I hadn't been steering, she'd have slammed into every table leg and tripped over every toy she had. But with me there, it was all good. I'd be steering at the console while I talked it out.

"Very nice," I'd say. "Okay, looks like you got this. Very good. Whoa, whoa, whoa, *whoa* . . . sharp turn . . . look out! Look out!"

There was always stuff just waiting around to jump out and skin Riley's knee. But I was a pro at keeping Riley safe. She never got hurt with me around. Well, she did get some scrapes from hockey. I warned everyone time and time again that hockey is a *contact sport*! People lose teeth playing that game! It was not a safe choice!

I was outvoted, though. And Riley did love hockey, so she was bruised and scraped but happy.

Then came the move to San Francisco, which is a major city where crime rates are far higher than those in our little Minnesota town, and where the percentage of dot-com people pretty much guarantees that cybercrime will be a part of Riley's life. Oh, and three more things:

Earthquakes—Earthquakes—*EARTHQUAKES!*

Why would Riley's parents want to live in a place where the very ground could break open and swallow them up?

I didn't have a say, though, so we left.

And the result was far, far worse than I'd feared. Dad drove an average of ten miles above the speed limit the entire way to San Francisco, which exponentially increased our chances of vehicular death. He and Mom wouldn't let Riley open the window because they wanted to keep the air-conditioning in, even though recycled car air increases the likelihood of passing airborne viruses from one passenger to another.

Then we got to our new house, even though "new" was a misnomer, as the house had obviously been lived in by people who clearly didn't clean up after themselves, and who could have left any number of germs and viruses on every surface.

Disgust and I were equally thrilled about that. The floors were also very creaky, and I'm fairly sure the house didn't have the superstructure to withstand . . . oh, an *earthquake*!

Joy tried to make us feel better about the house, but when Disgust gasped, "Is that a dead mouse?!" I knew we were in the wrong place. Dead rodents can carry viruses that are incredibly lethal!

Once again, Joy jumped in and reminded us the place would look better with Riley's things, and I could imagine that. I could picture her hockey lamp on her bedside table, tethered down so it didn't fall on Riley's bed during an earthquake. And I could imagine her posters stuck on the walls with double-sided tape—not pins. Pins could become dangerous projectiles or stick Riley's fingers while she was using them. The more I thought about it, the less I hyperventilated, and that was good.

Then Dad said the moving van was lost and wouldn't show up for a couple days.

Back to hyperventilating.

"The van is lost?!" I wailed. "This is the worst

day ever. San Francisco is terrible. And Mom and Dad are stressed out—even worse!"

Then there was the pizza debacle. There's nothing more frightening than finding a small tree on an otherwise perfectly normal plate of food, but that's exactly what happened. Riley and Mom went to the nearest pizza place and found *broccoli* on the pizza. I was terrified. If a pizza could have broccoli, it could have *anything*. It could have anchovies. Or liverwurst. Or roadkill.

Again, Joy calmed the rest of us down. She's really good at that. That's why she's usually the one driving. She showed us memories of Riley and our trip, and I was especially calmed when I remembered that Riley, Mom, and Dad all stayed securely belted into their seats the whole trip. That was important. But when the memory we were watching turned blue, I froze.

Not literally. It wasn't cold or anything, although there *is* a lot of fog in San Francisco, which is both cold *and* dangerous. What I'm saying is that I froze with fright because I've never seen a memory turn blue before. And I don't know about you, but I prefer only seeing things that I *have* seen before. That way I know if they're good or bad. New things are way too unpredictable and are far too likely to be dangerous.

I turned around and saw that Sadness was touching the memory. "She did something to the memory!" I said.

Joy did the right thing. She stepped in and took the memory away from Sadness, but the sphere stayed blue.

"Oh . . . change it back, Joy!" I urged her.

She tried to rub the blue off but couldn't, which meant the memory would stay sad forever.

Sadness never had that kind of power before. What did it mean? Had Sadness become a monster? Would she start turning all of Riley's memories blue? Would she turn *us* blue?

It seemed to me that Sadness was suddenly very dangerous. And she proved it only a minute later. Riley was about to do one of her favorite things . . . slide down a railing! I know, it's totally unsafe and not on my approved activities list. So I was secretly pleasantly surprised when Riley suddenly decided to forego the railing and walk down the stairs. But it wasn't my doing.

"Wait, what?" Joy asked. "What happened?"

I saw it at the same time Joy did. A core memory—one of the main memories that makes Riley who she is and powers her Islands of Personality—rolled on the floor and stopped at Joy's feet!

"A core memory!" I screamed.

"Oh, no," Joy gasped.

And it wasn't just any core memory—it was the one that powered Goofball Island, which had gone dark. That's why Riley hadn't slid. She couldn't be a goofball without Goofball Island. And even though I appreciated that she'd be safer if she never acted like a goofball, that wasn't Riley!

I watched Joy run to the core memory holder. Sadness was standing next to it.

"Sadness!" Joy snapped. "What are you doing?"

"It looked like one was crooked," Sadness said,

"so I opened it and then it fell out! I . . ."

Joy got the memory back in place and Goofball Island lit up again. Riley happily slid down the railing, but I was worried. Why was Sadness messing with important core memories? She wouldn't stop, either! When Joy asked why she did it, Sadness said, "I wanted maybe to touch one." And even as she said it, she reached out to a core memory and it *started to turn blue*! She was tainting the core memory! Who can function with tainted memories?

I was not okay with that. Not okay at all. I figured it was something about San Francisco. Maybe Sadness was allergic to the place. Maybe that's why she was acting so strange.

San Francisco wasn't suiting Mom and Dad, either. They both sounded so upset when they talked about the missing moving van or Dad's work . . . I didn't like it. I didn't like staying in Riley's new room with the ceiling that sloped down like a snowy mountain right before an avalanche. And I didn't like sleeping on the creaky floor in a thin sleeping bag that had been in storage for so long it was probably teeming with bedbugs. Did you know that mattresses get heavier over time because they fill with dust mites and dead skin? It's true! And I bet the same thing happens with sleeping bags. We were probably cuddled up with hordes of mites, all of which were just waiting to jump out and bite us in the middle of the night. And what about the weird glow of lights zipping across the room? Were they just cars passing by on the street, or were they something more sinister? And what about all the weird night noises? How did we know San Francisco didn't have bears?

"This move has been a bust," Anger said that first night, and I agreed.

"That's what I've been telling you guys!" I said. "There are at least thirty-seven things for Riley to be scared of right now!"

"The smell alone is enough to make her gag," said Disgust.

"Look, I get it," said Joy. "But we've been through worse! Tell you what: let's make a list of all the things Riley should be HAPPY about."

Well, none of us could think of a single happy thing. But Joy wouldn't give up.

"Okay, I admit it," she said. "We had a rough start. But think of all the good things that—"

"No, Joy," Anger snapped. "There's absolutely no reason for Riley to be happy right now. Let us handle this."

"I say we skip school tomorrow and lock ourselves in the bedroom," I said. It seemed like a great idea to me. Then Riley's bedroom door creaked open. Was it a psycho killer? The world's biggest dust mite?

No, it was Mom. She came in to thank Riley for being such a happy kid and making the move easier.

So I guess Joy knew what she was doing, even if I couldn't always see it right away. But we were on board and ready to support her. From then on, we'd be Team Happy! (Yep, I came up with the name by myself . . . not to brag or anything.)

The next day was the first day at the new school, and Joy had jobs for all of us. Mine was making a list of the possible negative outcomes on the first day of school, but Joy didn't realize I'd been working on that since the moment we had left Minnesota. I was on page fifty, and I really felt like I had only scratched the surface.

Oooh, scratched. Scratching. Itching. *Hives!* We could get *hives* on the first day of school!

I added that to the list. I felt pretty prepared, but when it came to the moment to walk into school, I lost my nerve.

"Are you sure we want to do this?" I asked Joy.

"In we go!" she demanded.

"Okaaaay!" I agreed. "Going in! Yes."

By the time we got to class, I was ready to make my full report to Joy. "Almost finished with the potential disasters," I told her. "Worst scenario is either quicksand, spontaneous combustion, or getting called on by the teacher. So as long as none of those happen . . ."

"Okay, everybody," Riley's teacher said. "We have a new student in class today."

"Are you kidding me?" I wailed. "Out of the

gate? This is not happening!"

"Riley," the teacher kept going, "would you like to tell us something about yourself?"

"Nooooo!" I screamed. "Pretend we can't speak English!"

Joy didn't listen to me. She took the controls, and she was going to get Riley through it just fine. At least, it seemed that way. Joy even took out a memory for Riley to think about to help her talk about home, which was really nice. It was a memory of Riley skating with Mom and Dad on our favorite frozen lake. As I watched Riley handle everything on the view screen in Headquarters, I almost forgot how terrified I was.

Then the image on the screen turned blue.

Uh-oh. Bad. Very bad. And wrong. What was going on? We all turned around and saw that Sadness had her hand on the memory. I had wondered up until then if Sadness had undergone some horrific transformation. Now I knew for sure she had turned. Sadness had become a MEMORY-CHANGING MONSTER!

Riley's happy memory from home had turned completely blue and sad, and the more Riley thought about it, the more upset she got.

"Get it out of there, Joy!" I demanded.

Joy tried to wrench the memory from the projector, but she couldn't. Meanwhile, everyone in class was staring at Riley like she was from another planet!

"Did you see that look?" I shouted frantically. "They're judging us!"

Disgust, Anger, and I all tried to help Joy remove the memory, but it wouldn't budge. It was like Sadness had put some kind of superglue spell on it.

"Everything's different now," Riley said as she kept talking to her class. "Since we moved . . ."

And then I saw it. The worst thing imaginable.

"Oh, no!" I wailed. "We're crying at *school!*"

I ran in wild circles. If I kept moving, maybe I could run so fast I could turn back time and none of this would have happened. The only thing that made me stop was the sound of a new memory sphere rolling into Headquarters.

It was a blue memory. And it was rolling toward the core memory holder.

"It's a core memory!" I gasped.

We'd *never* had a blue core memory. I could tell Joy didn't like it any more than I did, because she fought to keep it from getting into the holder while Sadness fought to get it *in* the holder.

I hate fighting. Fighting leads to injury, which leads to infection, which leads to death. But I wanted Joy to win this one. Instead, nobody won, because as they fought, they jostled the core memory holder and *all five core memories* . . .

I can't even say it. It's too terrible to even put into print.

Okay, I'll say it, but I warn you, I'm writing this with my eyes closed so I don't have to see the words.

ALL FIVE CORE MEMORIES SPILLED OUT!

Translation? ARMAGEDDON!

Everything that happened next was a blur, mainly because I went into a semi-unconscious state to deal with the stress. I know Joy went after the yellow core memories, and I heard Sadness shouting about her blue core memory, and then there was some accident with the vacuum tube, and then my entire life flashed before my eyes, and then I heard some more shouts and screams, and then I nearly passed out so I had to put my head between my knees for a second . . .

. . . and then it was all over.

Sadness, Joy, and the core memories had been sucked away.

Without the core memories to power them, the Islands of Personality went dark.

Life as we knew it had come to an abrupt end.

I did the only reasonable thing to do. I curled into a ball, shut my eyes, and wished the day away.

I felt very good about that decision. It seemed like the mature, sane way to handle things.

Anger and Disgust, however, didn't agree. They got me to my feet and, after Riley sat back down in her seat, I started driving the console. Riley slouched in her chair and hid behind a big text book. I wanted her to stay there for the rest of the day. Well, maybe not there, but possibly *under* her desk, which would give her protection in case of an earthquake—but apparently we had to get up and get through the rest of the school day *without Joy's help!*

Personally, I think we did okay. Riley was able to avoid interaction with all the kids and faculty—the last thing we wanted to do was talk to someone after what had happened. She wisely walked down the middle of each hallway, so the lockers wouldn't fall on her if there was an earthquake. She survived lunch without getting poisoned. She was able to find the one stall in the bathroom that was relatively clean. And she used that antibacterial stuff every time she went back to her locker (which had cobwebs in the corners—*cobwebs*).

Once school was over and we were away from all those prying kid eyes, I felt a little better. Well, not better—I actually felt worse than ever—but I felt *responsible*. Without Joy, the three of us left inside Headquarters had to step it up. And I, as the most brilliant of the three remaining Emotions, just happened to have a genius idea.

"Until Joy gets back, we just do what Joy would do."

We'd been with Riley a very long time. We could handle this. When Mom told us about a junior hockey league in San Francisco and asked Riley what she thought, I gave some sage advice.

"You pretend to be Joy," I said as I pushed Disgust up to the console.

She rolled her eyes at me, then put her hands on the controls.

"Won't it be great to be back out on the ice?" Mom asked Riley.

"Oh, yeah," Riley said, rolling her eyes. "That sounds fantastic."

"What was that?" I scolded her. "That wasn't anything like Joy."

"Uh, because I'm *not* Joy," she said.

"Yeah, no kidding," I shot back, which I guess was the wrong thing to say because then she pushed *me* to the console and said, "*You* pretend to be Joy."

"What?" I said. "Uh . . . okay."

I know I said I was feeling responsible and all, but running the console under direct questioning from Mom was not my area of expertise. I tried, though. I took the controls, and when Mom asked about the first day of school, I tried to give as straightforward and brave an answer as I could.

"It was fine, I guess," I had Riley say. "I don't know."

"Oh, very smooth," Disgust said. "That was *just* like Joy."

She didn't have to be so mean about it. I was trying.

When Riley's parents had more questions, Anger took the console. I have to say, he was the least Joy-like of all of us.

"Riley, I do *not* like this new attitude," Dad said in response to Anger's steering.

"Oh, I'll show you attitude, old man," Anger said.

"No!" I warned him. "No, no, no. Breathe."

Anger was leading us down the path to "Getting in Trouble" and, along the way, we'd probably make a stop at "Disappointed in You." I didn't want to be anywhere near that horror.

"What is your problem?" Riley shouted at Dad. "Just leave me alone."

Uh-oh.

A minute later, Dad had sent Riley to her room.

What were we thinking?! There was no way we could handle being Riley's entire personality! Our whole world was going down in flames! *Flames!*

When Dad came to visit Riley before bed, I was sure he'd see right through us and realize our desperate state. But he didn't. He tried to make things better by acting goofy with Riley. Normally I'd think that was cute. This time, though, it wasn't cute at all, because Riley couldn't play along. Goofball Island was down. It was dark. So Riley didn't respond to Dad's silliness. She just lay still. And that was totally unlike her, which gave me a very bad feeling. I knew something terrible would happen . . . and it did.

Goofball Island crumbled to the ground.

"Oh, Joy, where are you?" I cried.

It was the beginning of the end. Sinking into despair seemed like a sound idea, but Disgust and Anger were able to keep going, so I did, too.

I even got excited when Meg chatted with Riley. The two had been friends and hockey teammates forever. Maybe talking to Meg would make everything all better!

Then Meg said something about a new girl on the hockey team. And how cool she was.

"A *new girl*?" I screeched. "Meg has a new friend already?"

If Meg could dump us, *anyone* could dump us. Riley might not have any more friends *ever*! How could we know anyone was a true friend if the one we'd thought we could count on could disappear that easily?

If Meg could replace us that quickly . . . maybe she had *never* been a friend at all!

The knowledge hit me like a ton of bricks, which was pretty much what Friendship Island became as it crumbled to pieces and disappeared into the Memory Dump.

After the Meg disaster, waking up to face another day of school seemed like a very bad idea. Why even try to go and make new friends when they'd only dump us one day? At first I wanted Riley to stay under the covers and play sick so Mom would take care of her, but then I thought about how the power of ideas is very strong, and if Riley *said* she was sick, she might *become* sick, and then we'd have to deal with a cold on top of everything else!

So we went to school. Disgust had Riley's nose in a book most of the day to show she didn't need anyone else. That took care of the friend thing. And to make her seem even less approachable, Anger had caused a bit of a meltdown in computer class. The other kids must've thought Riley was nuts!

But, honestly, none of this really concerned me too much. I was preoccupied with all the potential disasters at this school! At one point Riley noticed that one of the fluorescent lights in math class was flickering. Not only did it give the whole room a creepy vibe, it was really bad for our eyesight. No one should have to multiply fractions in poor lightning conditions.

And then there was the girl who was sitting beside us in history class. She was secretly painting her nails an awful bloody red color under her desk. The nail polish she was using smelled terrible! Those fumes, especially in an enclosed classroom, were sure to be toxic! Riley wanted to open a window, but thought it was best not to draw attention to herself. So she just sat there inhaling the formaldehyde, which was probably killing tens of thousands of brain cells every second.

And just when we thought we had escaped the dangers of the day, Riley spotted the most horrific thing of all! A janitor was waxing the floor. *Waxing* it! Do you know how slippery floors are when they're waxed? She could easily fall and break a leg just getting to class!

I was thrilled to get out of that place, but after school we had even more problems. Mom took

Riley to tryouts for a hockey league. Riley still had Hockey Island, but without the core memory, it wasn't powered up. There was no way she'd be able to play the way she used to. I was terrified of what might happen. I didn't even want to imagine losing another island. I knew I had to do something. Then I had a brilliant idea!

"I've recalled every hockey memory I can think of," I told Anger and Disgust. The three of us were practically swimming in hockey-oriented memory spheres. I figured one of them could work in place of the core memory. I just had to load them into the core memory holder and see which ones took. I waited until Riley was about to play, then I started shoving the spheres inside the holder.

It worked! Oh, sure, Hockey Island was struggling and sputtering, but it was starting up and Riley was playing!

"We did it!" I cheered. "It's working—"

That's when the core memory holder blew out the memory spheres, slamming one into Anger's stomach.

I still thought we could make it work. I tried jamming another memory into the holder, but that one shot out like a cannon and slammed me into a wall. I was hurting, but I could see on the screen that Riley was doing even worse. Nothing worked for her on the ice, and the coach was really coming down on her. Anger didn't like it one bit. He stormed to the controls.

No good would come of Anger taking the console right then.

"Wait," I said. "No, no, no! Use your words."

He wouldn't. I knew he wouldn't. I threw myself on him to keep him away, but he's a lot stronger than I am, and he has that fire brewing on the top of his head, and that rage of his packs a lot of power, you know? Plus, I bruise very easily. I have to be careful.

What I'm saying is, I didn't win the battle for the controls. Anger steered, Riley raged at the coach, at Mom, at the entire sport of hockey . . . and the next thing I knew, Hockey Island was sinking like the *Titanic.*

By that night, I couldn't take it anymore. I wanted to quit, and I said as much to Anger and Disgust. "Sure, it's the coward's way out," I admitted. "But this coward is gonna survive."

I stomped on the memory flush button and a vacuum tube lowered. I wasn't sure where the tube would take me, but if it had whisked Joy and Sadness away from Headquarters, it could whisk me away from my troubles, too.

Unfortunately, the tube sucked up a memory sphere at the same time it sucked *me*. And it wasn't wide enough for the two of us. I ended up mushed against the side of the tube, the memory squeezing into my back. Then the tube spit me out onto the floor where I landed in a crumpled heap.

Ow.

"Aha!" Anger cried. He had been rummaging through a bunch of idea bulbs, and now he held one up triumphantly.

"What is it?" I asked.

"Oh, nothing . . . just the best idea ever," Anger declared.

"What?" Disgust scoffed.

"All the good core memories were made in Minnesota," Anger said. "Ergo, we go back to Minnesota and make more. Ta-da!"

"Wait, wait. You're saying we run away?" I asked in disbelief.

That was exactly what Anger was talking about. I couldn't believe he was serious!

"Hey," said Anger, "our life was perfect until Mom and Dad decided to move to San Fran Stinktown."

"But it's just so . . . drastic! Shouldn't we sleep on it or something?" I asked.

I was on Dream Duty that night, and I honestly figured something pleasant from Dream Productions would help calm my nerves, and I'd be able to handle everything better in the morning. Anger and Disgust agreed we wouldn't decide anything until then, so later that night, after Riley shut her eyes and went to sleep, I settled in with a nice hot cup of tea—not too hot, wouldn't want to scald my tongue—for some relaxing viewing.

The dream that night wasn't one of the studio's best. They were reenacting Riley's meltdown in front of the class, but the woman playing the teacher was totally unbelievable. While the dream was supposed to be scary, and believe me, I know scary, this was nothing. It was full of old clichés I could see coming a mile away. The actress playing Riley was speaking in front of the class . . . and then her teeth fell out.

Of course they did. "Who writes this stuff?" I asked. "Let me guess, we have no pants on."

Sure enough, a second later, someone cried, "Hey, look! She came to school with no pants on!"

Amateurs. They should get me down there to write and direct. If they could only harness the intensity of my fears, they'd have an endless supply of scares.

I leaned back, eager to make fun of the rest of the dream, when something unexpected happened. A puppy came flouncing out onto the set. I was intrigued. The writers usually stayed pretty literal. This was a nice departure.

"Woo!" cried the dog—also a nice touch, making it a *talking* dog—"Let's party! Let's dance. Woo!"

The air filled with balloons and confetti. A puppy party in the middle of what was supposed to be a nightmare? I liked it! I bounced around in my seat to the music, then took a big happy sip of my tea . . .

. . . which I spit all over the console when the cute puppy *split in half*!

"Aaaaaah!" I screamed.

I wanted to close my eyes, but I couldn't. The confetti and balloons were still everywhere, but now the front half of the bisected puppy was racing around and chasing the bottom half. I felt the tea churn in my stomach.

"It's just a dream," I told myself. "It's just a dream, it's just a dream . . ."

A second later, a huge animal that was part cat and part elephant bounced in front of the screen. He leaned in close, like he was trying to steal my soul. "Hi, Riley, it's me!"

"Bing Bong?" I said in disbelief. That was Riley's

imaginary friend from when she was little. Okay, now the director was just getting crazy, which she proved by panning over a second later to Rainbow Unicorn eating a donut at a buffet table.

"Boo!" I yelled at the screen. "Pick a plot line."

Well, it didn't get any better. The dream turned into an inane dance party full of glitter, sheep, cupcakes, and that ridiculous Rainbow Unicorn. And just when I thought things couldn't get any worse . . . they did.

I was dozing off when a giant clown with a bloodthirsty red mouth and piercing evil eyes crashed through the set with a giant hammer.

"WHO'S THE BIRTHDAY GIRL?!" it roared.

I screamed so hard I blew out my voice . . . then I passed out. I don't even remember coming to. The next thing I knew, I was tucked under the console, rocking back and forth and hugging myself. That's where Anger and Disgust found me. I guess my screaming woke them up, and they were both so annoyed that they couldn't even get a good night's sleep anymore that they didn't want to wait until morning to decide about running away. They made the choice immediately. I didn't say no.

Anger plugged the idea bulb into the console, and that was that. Riley sat up in bed and pulled out her laptop to check bus schedules. Of course, she needed money to buy a ticket, but Anger reminded us that Mom had left her purse downstairs in the kitchen. I would have been far too afraid to take money, but Anger was driving now. He led Riley downstairs, had her pluck out Mom's credit card, and then snuck her back upstairs.

That made Honesty Island collapse. I was too overwhelmed to even flinch.

The following morning, as we loaded up Riley's backpack for school, I had second thoughts. "Hold on, guys," I said. "Are we really doing this?"

Anger pushed me away from the console. He thought running away was the only answer, and since I didn't have a better one, I let him steer. Riley left home without a single word to Mom and Dad and began walking toward the bus station. As she walked, I just couldn't stop thinking of all the terrible things that happen to kids who run away. We didn't even know where we were going! Getting lost was almost inevitable. Once we got off at the bus stop in Minnesota, where would we go? What would we do? Riley needed to get some maps of Minnesota—stat!

As she approached a public library, I took the console for a while. She walked right into the library and began looking for the maps. She didn't find a map, but she did find a Minnesota tour guidebook that had a ton of small maps and big pullout one. It was perfect! She headed for the checkout desk, but along the way I pushed a few buttons on the console. One more stop: the library catalog computers. Riley typed in "runaways" in the subject field and, moments later, the screen had a long list of book titles. I had no idea there were so many books about runaway kids! We went to the stacks to look at some of them. They were all so scary! Even the covers were terrifying . . . all these young boys and girls with terror in their eyes, backpacks slung over their shoulders, walking along shadowy roads . . . did we really want to be like them?

The worst part was the librarian. She kept coming over and asking if Riley needed help. And when she saw what kind of books we were looking at . . . I just knew she had our plan figured out, and she'd call Mom and Dad.

Incredibly, that didn't happen. Riley didn't waste another second and headed straight for the desk to check out the guidebook. (I was going to make sure she mailed it back to the library before the due date—we didn't want to get thrown in jail for overdue fees.)

As Riley scurried out of the library and continued on her way to the bus station, Anger resumed control of the console. It was a good thing he had the controls, because we had to go through a dimly lit part of town that had shadows in every corner. Shadows that could hold kidnappers . . . or muggers . . . or hyenas. I had images in my head of Riley ending up dead on the side of the road or having a really bad picture appear on the sides of milk cartons all over the country.

Mom called while we were walking. I knew Riley should answer, but I didn't want her to. I was too afraid to hear what Mom might say. Was she worried? Did she know Riley was running away? Oh, no! What if she could track us through Riley's phone? Maybe that would only work if we answered. Better not to answer. Better to just keep moving.

The station was filled with strangers. Not just strangers—*strange* strangers. I made sure we stayed in the most wide-open spaces we could find, and we made eye contact with no one.

Riley's phone rang.

"Oh . . ." I moaned. "It's Mom again. What do we do?"

Family Island made a loud groan as it started to topple.

"We're losing the last island!" Disgust cried.

Suddenly, Anger decided that running away was the worst idea ever.

Disgust reached for the idea bulb we'd plugged into the console. "Let's get that idea out of her head," she said.

She and Anger both tried, then Anger said, "It's stuck!"

"Whaddya mean it's stuck?" I asked.

Then all the controls started shutting down. A black shadow spread over the console, like an eclipse of tar.

"What is *this*?" I screeched.

Anger picked up a chair and manfully slammed it down on the console . . . but the chair bounced off and nearly hit me in the face, which wasn't quite the effect I wanted. I tried to attack the thing with a crowbar, but that didn't work, either. At least it wasn't just me.

"How do we stop it?" I asked.

"Make her feel scared!" Disgust suggested. "That'll make her change her mind!"

"Yes!" I cried. "Brilliant!"

I ran to the control panel and pushed every button. I tried to recall the scariest things she'd ever experienced: the food at camp, the cockroach she once found swimming in the toilet, that oversized Easter Bunny at the amusement park . . . but nothing worked. The console didn't even respond.

"Guys," I said, "I can't make Riley feel anything."

Everyone was silent for a moment, and for the first time, I think Anger and Disgust were as frightened as I always was.

"That's it," Anger said. "It's over. There's nothing more to do."

He was right. The world was ending, and it was punctuated with a horrible banging sound against the window. It was over. Headquarters was falling apart. The walls around us were collapsing! We would all be buried alive!

"It's Joy!" Disgust shouted.

What? Joy? *Joy* was back?

That was amazing! Life wasn't over after all!

I ran to the window and saw Joy and Sadness clinging to the outside. Disgust, Anger, and I tried to open it, but the thing was made of safety glass, which I'd always loved. It wouldn't budge—not even when Anger threw a chair at it and tried to break it. Then the wheels started turning in Disgust's head. She insulted Anger until he fumed so violently that flames burst from the top of his head. Then she used him like a blowtorch to cut a hole in the window. Joy and Sadness were finally able to climb inside Headquarters.

"Thank goodness you're back!" I cried.

Joy didn't even answer. She just looked at the screen and saw that Riley was on the bus, and the bus driver was pulling away.

For the first time in ages, I wasn't worried. I knew Joy would handle everything and make Riley happy again.

But she didn't.

"Sadness," she said, "it's up to you."

What? Did Joy go crazy as she was wandering out there in the Mind World? What was she talking about? Sadness couldn't make things better. She's the one who started this whole mess by turning Riley's memories from happy to sad. Letting Sadness take control was dangerous. Yet Joy didn't seem worried. If anything, *Sadness* looked nervous and worried, but she took the console.

I concentrated on my breathing as I watched the screen. It only took a few moments before Riley suddenly stood up from her seat, raced to the front of the bus, and told the driver to stop. With Sadness still at the controls, Riley ran home and told her parents exactly how she felt about the move, and how sad she was to leave behind her old friends and the home she loved.

The truth? I kind of teared up listening to her.

I was afraid Mom and Dad wouldn't understand, or would be mad at her for not being the happy kid they loved . . . but they only hugged Riley. They said they were sad, too. At that moment, a new core memory was formed, and it created a new Family Island. Riley was healing already.

That was a while back. Now we have an amazing new view from Headquarters. We can see all the new Islands of Personality. They're pretty spectacular. All except Boy Band Island—that one is just plain annoying. But the really great thing is that Joy, Sadness, Anger, Disgust, and I work together now at a cool new console. Sure, it can get a little crowded sometimes, and I always risk getting singed by Anger or sobbed on by Sadness, but it's worth it. We're a team, and there's nothing scary about that—well, other than the possibility of a meteor striking when we're all standing together.

Anger

Okay, listen up and listen good, because this is important. I don't know what any of these other Emotions have said, but I'm going to tell you the *real* story of the disaster that was Riley's Big Move, and I'm going to tell it exactly the way it happened so everyone knows the truth.

It started, of course, with me. I showed up in Riley's life pretty early. You know why? Because life isn't fair. But when people try to make it not fair to Riley, I fight back. Even when Riley was a toddler, there was unfairness to be dealt with. Take this for example: Dad used to tell Riley that if she didn't eat her dinner, she wasn't going to have any dessert.

Excuse me? No *dessert*? That move didn't fly with me. I was *not* above having Riley throw a tantrum to get what she wanted. Trust me on this: sometimes a tantrum is what it takes.

I should have had her throw a tantrum when we heard about moving from Minnesota to San Francisco. But no, I believed Joy when she said Mom and Dad knew what they were doing and it would all be fine. WRONG!

The car ride to California was cramped and long; the food on the road made Riley's stomach hurt; the music Dad played was boring and for old people; and to top it all off, when we finally got to San Francisco, the house was disgusting!

"We're supposed to live here?" I roared to Joy.

She said the house might be a disappointment, but Riley's room would be wonderful.

WRONG AGAIN!

"Get out the rubber ball," I said when I saw the tiny slope-roofed cell. "We're in solitary confinement."

And you know what happened from there? It

got worse. The moving van with all our stuff got lost. Our brilliant leader, Joy—please note my sarcasm—thought pizza would make us feel better, which it would have *if there were such a thing as pizza in that godforsaken town!* The pizza place Riley and Mom went to gave us some garbage with broccoli on it and called it "pizza." The flames were starting to flare up on my head.

"Congratulations, San Francisco," I roared. "You've *ruined pizza!* First the Hawaiians and now *you!*"

Unreal. Oh, sure, Joy showed Riley and the rest of us some memories that made us feel better for a second, but that blew up in her face when Sadness touched the memory spheres and turned them blue. Yeah, that's right—Joy tried to cheer up Riley with a memory that was suddenly a *sad* memory. How was that gonna work? And it wasn't like Sadness's blue tinge on the memory spheres was temporary. Oh, no. The blue was on it *for good.*

But, hey, turning happy memories sad was apparently only one of Sadness's new skills. Know

Driven By Emotions

what the other one was? *Destroying Islands of Personality!*

Okay, not *destroying* them—not yet, anyway—but while Joy was trying her whole shiny-scrubby thing on the memory Sadness had tainted, Sadness decided to open up the core memory holder. She thought the memories were crooked, she said. She wanted to straighten them out, she said. Well, she straightened one out all right. She straightened it right out of the holder! It was the core memory that powered Goofball Island, and when it rolled onto the floor, the island went dark!

Guess how much good a dark island does Riley? DING, DING, DING! That's right, folks—NONE!

That night, I said what everyone else was thinking but was afraid to say. "I can't believe Mom and Dad moved us here. They must suffer for this!"

Joy tried to do her little "think of the good things" song and dance, but I was having none of it.

"No, Joy," I told her. "There's absolutely no reason for Riley to be happy right now. Let us handle this."

I wasn't sure yet *how* we were going to handle it, although a bulldozer or sledgehammer seemed like a good place to start.

Then Mom came in and was all lovey-dovey happy because Riley's upbeat nature made the stressful move easier on everyone. It was . . . well, you know . . . kind of nice. I told Joy I never doubted her for a second, which was a bald-faced lie, but I guessed I owed her a little pat on the back. And for a half a second I was even optimistic. Maybe things *would* turn around in this place.

Nope, they would not.

The next day was the first day of school, and it started off disastrous because Joy pranced around playing her accordion, an instrument that is, by definition, a crime against music. Then she started doling out jobs. Mine was to unload daydreams Joy had ordered in case things got slow in class. Want to know what *my* dream was? That I'd never have to see another "flying pony" daydream. Although if school ended up being really boring and useless, which it probably would be, one of those ridiculous ponies might actually come in handy.

Riley got to school and it seemed to go okay at first. She got to class, sat down, blended in . . . all good. Then the teacher, who I swear must have run a prison camp before she earned her teaching credentials, thought it would be a fine idea to have the new kid get up and talk to everyone. Fine. Joy handled it and Riley started out okay. We were all watching her on the big screen when, out of nowhere, the screen started to turn blue. I turned around and saw Sadness touching the memory Joy had recalled for Riley to talk about.

The gall of Sadness! What right did she have to change memories? Joy grabbed the sphere, but it wouldn't come out of its spot, which meant Riley couldn't stop thinking about it. And since the memory was sad now, Riley got more and more upset.

Well done, Sadness. Way to ruin the already horrible institution of school.

Fear, Disgust, Joy, and I all tried to dislodge the memory, but it wouldn't move. What *did* move was a new memory that rolled into Headquarters. It was a miserable *blue* memory that rolled toward the core memory holder.

You know what that means, right? It was a sad core memory! Imagine the island that it would create. Chronic Depression Island, maybe, or Cry Me to Sleep Island. Oh, what a lovely place it would be. Who knows . . . it might even come with an ocean of tears!

Naturally, Joy tried to keep the memory out of the core memory holder. Sadness tried to get it in. Fighting ensued, but it wasn't the good kind of fighting with wrestlers in an arena body-slamming one another. It was a pitiful kind of fighting that only succeeded in dumping all five core memories onto the floor when Sadness and Joy bumped the holder.

That's right, you heard me. They dumped the core memories. And then those two geniuses managed to get themselves *and* the memories sucked up into a vacuum tube and disappeared, leaving me, Fear, and Disgust to pick up the slack.

Oh, yeah, and with the core memories gone, all the Islands of Personality went dark. Nice, right?

So the three of us got Riley through the rest of the school day. Let me tell you a little bit about Riley's new school. First of all, whoever decorated the school did so blindfolded. The color scheme in the halls was a mix of pastel green and yellow. Riley overheard one of the teachers calling it "soothing." Soothing? It looked like someone threw up banana all over a meadow. You know what else wasn't soothing? Looking out the window and seeing nothing but thick gray fog. You know what was outside the windows in Minnesota? *Sky! Sun! White puffy clouds!* Here our entire building may as well have been stuffed inside a pillow.

Then lunch. Don't even get me started on lunch. The motto for San Francisco should be "Peace, Love, and Broccoli." Massive, steaming piles of broccoli were spooned out onto all the kids' plates. Even if you didn't take the broccoli, you might as well have, because the smell of broccoli was everywhere! The tortilla soup smelled like broccoli, the fruit cup smelled like broccoli . . . Riley even went to check out the optional peanut butter and jelly table, and the *peanut butter* smelled like broccoli.

I couldn't have been happier when school was over, but going home and having dinner with Mom and Dad wasn't much better. Instead of letting Riley enjoy her meal in peace, Mom was yammering on about some junior hockey league.

"Hockey?!" I blurted. I mean come on—like *hockey* was the most important thing right now. It didn't even make the top thousand. Fear and Disgust tried to handle the conversation, but Mom knew something was weird.

"So," she said in this fake-casual tone of voice, "how was the first day of school?"

"She's probing us," I warned.

Fear gave some kind of half-witted answer, but that just brought Dad into the conversation. Soon he was probing, too, and exchanging knowing little glances with Mom. I hate those knowing little glances.

"Move," I said, pushing Fear out of the way. "*I'll be Joy.*" I took the controls on the console and dialed up Riley's snark factor.

"School was great," she sneered, "all right?"

"Riley," Mom asked, "is everything okay?"

Right, because Riley can't be anything but sunny all the time, and if she's not, something has to be seriously wrong. Which it was, of course, but Mom didn't *know* that for sure.

"Uggghhhh," Riley groaned.

"Riley, I do *not* like this new attitude," Dad said.

Attitude? He thought *that* was an attitude? "Oh, I'll show you attitude, old man," I said.

"What is your problem?" Riley shouted at Dad. "Just leave me alone."

Dad thought he'd take the offensive after that. "Listen, young lady," he said, "I don't know where this disrespectful attitude is coming from . . ."

"You want a piece of this, Pops?" I challenged him from the control panel. "Come and get it!" I pushed two levers forward as far as they could go, and Riley glared into Dad's eyes.

ANGER

"Yeah?" she prodded him. "Well . . . well . . ."

I pushed down on a third lever and screamed until my head burst into flames.

"Just shut up!" Riley yelled.

Atta girl.

Yeah, Riley got sent to her room, but I still felt good about it. Dad must have known we were right, too, because he came up later to try and make things better. Unfortunately, he started making monkey noises, which would have made Riley laugh if Goofball Island was operational—but it wasn't. Riley couldn't be a goofball, so she just shut her mouth and ignored him, which was so unlike Riley that it made Goofball Island crumble to dust.

But, hey, we could do without Goofball if we had to. We had other islands. At least we did until later, when Riley's "friend" Meg called her on her laptop. Did you note the quotation marks around the word "friend"? Yeah, that was on purpose. This "friend" had the nerve to talk to Riley about a new friend. Actually, make that a new BFF, who was so in sync with Meg on the hockey rink that they could practically read one another's minds!

"You like to read minds, Meg?" I roared. "I got something for you to read right here!"

I took the controls, and Riley slammed the laptop shut. Meg must have been stunned. It was totally satisfying. And if that was what made Friendship Island crumble, then it wasn't my fault, it was that little traitor Meg's.

Apparently Fear, Disgust, and I were playing a game of Knock Down the Personality Islands, but again, not our fault. We weren't the ones who were supposed to be in charge, and we certainly weren't the ones who let the core memories out of their holder. We were only playing the hand we were dealt, which is exactly what we kept on doing the next day at school.

For the most part, the day was tolerable. Riley pretended to read a book so everyone would just leave her alone. And if anyone was considering coming up to Riley that day, they got the message to back off after computer class. That's when Riley got upset. Hey, you would, too, if you had to deal with a swirling rainbow of doom on your computer screen! ARGHHHHHHH! Is anything more frustrating than that? Anyway, the other kids gave us a wide berth after that one, which was fine with me because I was not in the mood for anyone getting in Riley's face and pretending to be all nicey-nicey-what's-wrong. They might seem like they were being friendly, but they'd only be stringing us along until they found someone better, just like Meg had.

After school that day, Mom took Riley to tryouts for a hockey league. I knew it was a terrible idea, and I made sure Riley kept a grousy look on her face so Mom knew it, but it didn't help. Fear had this whackadoodle idea that a hockey tryout could go just fine even with Hockey Island dark. He recalled all of Riley's hockey memories and tried to use them as replacement core memories.

Hey, fine, I'm a team player. I didn't think it would work, but I went along with the plan. As Riley started playing, ! tried shoving the memories into the core memory holder, struggling to make them

Driven By Emotions

fit. But then one of the memory spheres flew out of the holder and rocketed right into my gut. *OOF!*

While I was killing myself to make Hockey Island work, Riley was getting pulverized on the ice. And her ridiculous coach started taunting her, pushing her to play better, like she wasn't doing the best she could.

Not acceptable. Let Disgust and Fear shove ill-fitting spheres into the core memory holder. I was going to drive the console. Riley wasn't going to put up with this nonsense anymore. As I pounded some buttons and jammed a lever, Riley threw her stick on the ice and skated off the rink. Then she huffed to Mom that she was done and stormed out of the building.

Did Hockey Island crumble? Yes, it did. Was it at all my doing? No, Your Honor, it was not.

The three of us were on a sinking ship, and things were only getting worse. So that night, I tried to take charge. "Well, why don't we quit standing around and do something?" I asked Disgust and Fear.

ANGER

Fear said we should quit, but he just meant he wanted to suck himself into a tube like Sadness and Joy had. He didn't realize what he was actually saying. I did, though, and it reminded me of an idea that we had tucked away for occasions just like this one.

"Wait a minute," I said. "Wait a minute!"

I rummaged through the idea bulbs until I found what I was looking for. *"Aha!"* I cried.

"What is it?" Fear asked.

"Oh, nothing. Just the best idea ever," I replied as I held up the idea bulb for everyone to see. "All the good core memories were made in Minnesota. Ergo, we go back to Minnesota and make more. Ta-da!"

"You can't be serious," Fear said.

Fear clearly didn't know me at all. "Hey," I said. "Our life was perfect until Mom and Dad decided to move to San Fran Stinktown."

"But, it's just so . . . drastic!" said Fear.

"Need I remind you of how great things were there?" I asked, though apparently I did. Fear was completely clueless. "Our room? Our backyard? Our friends?"

Fear and Disgust weren't sold, which made no earthly bit of sense to me, but I told them we could sleep on it. "Because, hey," I said sarcastically, "I'm sure jolly, fun-filled times are just around the corner."

I don't know what the heck happened that night. All I know is I was asleep, enjoying a moment of peace and quiet, and the next thing I knew, Fear was screaming and Riley was bolting awake in bed. And when Riley was up, we were all up. I stormed into Headquarters from the break room, cranky from the lack of sleep, and there was Fear, huddled under the console in a trembling ball of humiliation. Disgust asked him what was going on, and he started babbling about half a dog, no pants, and Riley's old imaginary friend Bing Bong. . . .

"You idiot!" I yelled. "It was a *dream*! This is ridiculous; we can't even get a good night's sleep anymore. Time to take action." I grabbed the idea bulb I'd found earlier. "Stupid Mom and Dad," I grumbled. "If they hadn't moved us, none of this would have happened." I took the idea to the console and held it up. "Who's with me?"

Fear just babbled, but Disgust gave the go-ahead. That was good enough for me. I plugged the idea into the console. Almost immediately, Riley got out of bed and turned on her computer.

"She took it," I said. "There's no turning back."

Disgust, in her infinite wisdom, asked how we'd get to Minnesota from San Francisco.

"Well," I said, "why don't we go to the elephant lot and rent an elephant?"

"That sounds nice," said Fear.

"We're taking the bus, nitwit!" I snapped.

I watched as Riley checked the schedule on her computer. "There's a bus leaving tomorrow," I noted. "Perfect."

Then Disgust asked about money for the ticket. Like I hadn't already thought of that.

"Mom's purse," I said.

"You wouldn't," she gasped, but I assured her that, indeed, I would. I even called up a memory so we could recall where Mom had left her purse—downstairs. "Mom and Dad got us into this mess," I reminded Disgust and Fear. "They can pay to get us out."

Sneaking downstairs and "borrowing" the credit card was shockingly easy. Watching Honesty Island topple was a lot harder, though. But I knew once we got back to Minnesota we'd be able to build new Islands of Personality, and Riley would be herself again.

Fear got nervous the next morning as we were getting ready to go, but I wasn't going to hear any excuses. If we wanted to make life better, we had to do something. I took the console, and Riley was soon filling her backpack with clothes. Then we walked out the front door and took our first steps to freedom. I steered Riley through some nasty parts of town. Then Fear took over and led us to a library, which was a big waste of time. He said he wanted to be prepared for the worst. But we just ended up reading lame books about lame runaways. Riley was so much stronger and smarter than those kids. She'd be fine! I'd make sure of it.

I took the console again, and we resumed our journey to the bus station. Riley just kept her head down and kept walking. She looked tough—no one was going to mess with her!

Then Mom called Riley's cell phone, but Riley refused to answer.

We were on a mission, and we were going to see it through. I was sure of that right up until we got close to the ticket booth at the bus station. Then I started thinking of Mom . . . and Dad . . . and how much they'd miss us . . . and how awful it would be for Riley to be alone.

"This is madness!" I yelled. "What are we thinking? She shouldn't run away."

Fear and Disgust felt the same way. We all tried to get the running away idea out of the console, but it wouldn't move.

"It's stuck!" I yelled.

It was worse than stuck. It was burning up. The idea got so hot it seared Fear's hands when he touched it. That probably traumatized him for

Driven By Emotions

life. He won't be touching idea bulbs again anytime soon.

I then tried throwing a chair to dislodge the idea, but even that didn't do the trick. And then this crazy black shadow spread over the console. I had never seen anything like it before. It was completely destroying the console! Fear tried to scare Riley in hopes that would get the idea out of the console, but the controls were unresponsive.

"What have we done?" I asked.

But I knew what we'd done. We'd messed up. Royally.

When we heard something bang against the window of Headquarters, I figured the place was collapsing just like the islands. But for once, I'm happy to say I was wrong. Disgust ran to the window to check it out and cried, "It's Joy!"

We followed Disgust to the window, and there they were: Joy and Sadness, dangling from a ledge outside. Why they tried to come in that way I'll never know. The windows don't open, so there was no way to get them in. Oh, we tried. I even threw a

ANGER

chair at the window, but it just bounced off.

Then I had the most brilliant idea. Well, maybe it really wasn't my idea, but that doesn't matter. You know how I can make my head burst into flames? That's exactly what I did! I essentially became a blowtorch and cut a hole through the window! Then Joy and Sadness crawled through the hole and back into Headquarters.

Yep, I pretty much saved the day.

I'm sure you heard from the other Emotions what happened next. Joy let Sadness take the reins, blah, blah, blah, Sadness found her purpose and saved the day, blah, blah, blah, reconciliation with Mom and Dad, blah, blah, blah, Joy and Sadness BFFs.

I wasn't moved at all. NOT. AT. ALL. Okay, a little bit. But only because I love Riley, and afterwards I was *fine*, and no one even saw me cry. Didn't happen. They can't prove ANYTHING!

So it's been several months since all this went down, and I'm now a far more integral part of Riley's emotional life. We all are: the new core memories are multicolored now, as are most of the new memories. We even run the place at a new console that lets us all drive at once, which is pretty cool—especially when we play hockey. I'm the aggressive one, Fear looks out for defenders, Joy keeps us motivated, Sadness comes into play when we get hurt, and Disgust is more concerned about keeping Riley's sweat quotient down, but still, we make a really good team. I like it.

You want to know another great thing? Riley has some fresh Islands of Personality now, and some expansions of the old ones. My favorite? The new "Friendly Argument" section of Friendship Island. When that fires up, I'm so happy you could almost mistake me for Joy.

Almost . . . but not quite.

Sadness

Hi. Um . . . I don't really think you'll want to hear what I have to say . . . people usually don't. But I'm supposed to tell you about Riley moving to San Francisco from Minnesota and all the stuff that happened then, so I guess I will, but if you want to stop at any point and read one of the other Emotions telling their version of the story, I understand.

So . . . um . . . let's see. Where to start?

Well, I've always loved Riley. When she was just thirty-three seconds old, I helped her cry. She needed to cry. She had just popped into the world, and it was so big, and she was so small, and she was cold and hungry and needed someone to

Driven By Emotions

bundle her up. So she cried. And she got what she needed.

There are five of us Emotions inside Riley's head: me, Joy, Fear, Disgust, and Anger, but I always felt like the odd one out. I don't know why. I just did. And it made me sad. I felt like Joy especially didn't understand me, and since she was the one who always took charge, it was just easier to be by myself. Except when Riley needed me.

Then the move happened. I felt terrible leaving our old home in Minnesota, where we had so many memories, and I felt even worse when I saw our new house. It was so dark and dusty.

"Do we have to live here?" I asked.

Riley's room was small and cramped, too, and I almost cried when I thought of Riley shut away in there, but then Joy said we could decorate it and that sounded nice. But when we found out the moving van was missing, I was sure we'd never see it again, and that was almost unbearable.

"All our stuff is gone," I said. "I miss our clothes, our rainbow socks . . . everything."

SADNESS

San Francisco just seemed like the unhappiest place in the world. Dad was even more stressed there. And he had to leave during dinnertime. He never did that when we lived in Minnesota.

"He doesn't love us anymore," I told the other Emotions. "That's sad."

In fact, it felt so sad that I knew Riley needed me to drive the console. I walked over to take the controls, but Joy wouldn't let me.

"Joy, what are you doing?" I asked.

She said she should drive because we were going to have lunch, and that sounded like a fun thing, so I guessed that made sense. But it turned out lunch wasn't fun. It was a yucky pizza with broccoli. And when Riley and Mom got back home, Joy tried to cheer them up with happy memories, but I couldn't help feeling like I was supposed to be driving. Or if not driving, then at least I was supposed to be a part of the memory.

I stared at the sphere Joy had plugged in. I saw the memory on the screen, too. It was the time during the road trip when Dad accidentally let the car roll backward and it hit the tail of a cement dinosaur. It was funny . . . but to me it was sad, too, because that road trip was over, and now we were stuck in a place that was new and kind of creepy and where we didn't really belong.

I couldn't help myself. While everyone else was watching the memory, I moved closer and closer to the sphere . . . and then I touched it.

The screen turned blue.

How did that happen? I didn't mean for it to happen.

Everyone spun and looked at me. Then they looked at the sphere. I looked at it, too. It was *blue*. It wasn't just the screen that was blue, the *memory sphere* was blue. It was a sad memory now, even though it had been a happy memory before.

"What did you do?" Joy asked.

"I just touched it," I said.

Joy rubbed the memory. I guess she was trying to rub off the blue. But it wouldn't come off.

"That shouldn't make it change," Joy said.

She was right. I couldn't explain how it

happened. I felt bad because everyone was looking at me, and Disgust even said I did something bad by making the memory unhappy. Whenever Riley thought about that time with the dinosaurs, she'd feel sad now. Thanks to me.

"Don't touch any other memories until we figure out what's going on," Joy told me. I said okay, and I meant it . . . but when everyone went back to looking at Riley on the big screen in Headquarters, I noticed the core memory holder. There was something about it. One of the memories inside looked crooked. I knew I wasn't supposed to touch the memories. I'd promised Joy I wouldn't. Still, I couldn't help it. I needed to get into that core memory holder and straighten out the crooked memory. I just . . . I had to. I opened the holder and reached inside . . .

. . . and one of the core memories rolled out.

Uh-oh.

I wondered if I could slip the core memory back into the holder without anyone noticing, but it was already too late. Everyone was looking at me. They didn't look happy. I tried to explain, but what I said wasn't what I expected to say. It was more true.

"I wanted to maybe hold one," I admitted.

I still wanted to hold one. I reached out to one of the core memories in the holder and it started to turn blue. I felt like it was pulling me toward it. Like it wanted me to touch it.

"Whoa, whoa, *whoa!*" Joy said. She grabbed my hand so I couldn't touch it anymore. "Sadness, when I said don't touch any memories, that meant core memories *most of all!*"

She put the core memory that had fallen back into the holder. I hadn't even realized that when the memory fell out, Goofball Island had gone dark, but now I saw it light up again.

That was a relief. I wouldn't want Riley to lose any of her islands. I just wanted to do what the core memories wanted me to do. They wanted me to touch them. At least, that's how I felt. Didn't that mean it was true?

"I'm sorry," I told Joy. "Something's wrong with me. I, uh . . . it's like I'm having a breakdown."

"You're not having a breakdown," Joy said. "It's stress."

"I keep making mistakes like that," I said. "I'm awful . . ."

"Nooo, you're not," Joy said.

". . . and annoying," I added.

"Well, uh . . . eh . . . you know what?" Joy suggested. "You can't focus on what's going wrong. There's always a way to turn things around. To find the fun."

"Yeah," I said. I guessed that was true. "Find the fun. I don't know how to do that."

"Okay," Joy said, "well, try to think of something funny."

I thought hard. "Oh! Remember the funny movie where the dog dies?"

Joy didn't think that was funny, so she reminded me of the time Riley's best friend, Meg, made Riley laugh so hard milk came out of her nose.

"Yeah, that hurt," I said. "It felt like fire. Ooh, it was awful."

I got sad just thinking about how much it hurt.

I guess Joy wanted me to feel better, so she asked me about my favorite things to do.

"My favorite?" I asked. "Um, well, I like it when we're outside . . ."

"That's good," Joy said. "Like there's the beach and sunshine. Oh! Like that time we buried Dad in the sand up to his neck—"

"Oh," I said. "I was thinking more like rain."

Joy said she liked rain, too. She liked stomping around in puddles, cool umbrellas, and lightning storms.

I said I was thinking more about when the rain runs down Riley's back and makes her shoes soggy. She gets all cold and shivery, and everything just starts feeling droopy.

I started to cry.

"Oh, hey, hey, hey . . . easy," Joy said. "Why are you crying? Oh, it's . . . it's just like really the opposite of what we're going for here."

"Crying helps me slow down and obsess over the weight of life's problems," I told her.

That's when Joy told me I should sit by myself

and read some mind manuals. I'd read them all before, but I didn't want to disappoint Joy. It kinda seemed like I always disappointed her, so I wanted to try and be better. I settled in to do some reading.

Later, Mom came to kiss Riley good night. Mom said she was glad Riley was her happy self because it made the move so much better. All the other Emotions seemed to feel better when they heard that, and I did, too . . . but not really. Maybe I should have, but instead I just felt funny inside. Not funny ha-ha, but funny weird. Maybe I was still upset about the broccoli pizza Riley'd been served earlier, I didn't know . . . I just knew I felt off. I hoped maybe I'd go to sleep and wake up and everything would be better.

Joy seemed to think it was. She woke up and played her accordion and got all excited for the first day of school. She gave everyone jobs, too.

"Sadness, I have a super-important job just for you," she said.

That sounded exciting. "Really?" I asked.

"Mmm hmmm. Follow me," she said.

Joy led her to a spot in the very back of Headquarters, then knelt down on the floor.

"What are you doing?" I asked.

"There. Perfect," she said. She stood up, and I saw she'd drawn a chalk circle around my feet. "This is the Circle of Sadness," she said. "Your job is to make sure that all the Sadness stays inside of it."

"So . . . you want me to just stand here?" I asked. It didn't sound like much of a job.

"Hey," Joy said, "it's not *my* place to tell you how to do your job. Just make sure that *all* the Sadness stays in the circle."

She used her foot to nudge mine back inside the circle. I guess I'd let it slip outside the Circle of Sadness. I stood there and looked at Joy.

"See?" she said. "You're a pro at this! Isn't this fun?"

"No," I said.

"Atta girl," said Joy.

That is why sometimes I thought Joy didn't like me very much.

SADNESS

I tried to stay in my Circle of Sadness. I really did. I had never disobeyed Joy before, but . . .

You know how I said it was like the core memories wanted me to touch them? Well, as Riley went through her first day of school, I got that feeling again, more and more. And it wasn't just the core memories—I got the feeling that I was supposed to be steering. That even though Joy said this was a happy day . . . it wasn't. It was sad. And if it was sad, I needed to be at the controls.

Still, I stayed put while Riley got to school, while she walked into the building, while she sat at her desk. I even stayed still when the teacher asked her to introduce herself, and when Joy called up a memory for Riley to describe to all the other kids.

The memory was of Riley and her family skating together. It was a golden, happy memory, but it pulled me like a magnet because it needed me. It needed to be blue. It needed to be a little sad. After all, Riley wouldn't be able to skate like that anymore with Mom and Dad. They lived in San Francisco now, where it didn't even snow. So while the other Emotions were watching Riley on the big screen, I tiptoed to the memory sphere and touched it.

On the big screen, the image turned blue. Riley's voice got sad and small.

I felt awful when Joy spun around and saw me touching the memory. She looked really upset.

"Sadness!" she snapped. "You touched a memory? We talked about this."

"Oh, yeah, I know," I admitted. "I'm sorry."

"Get back in your circle," she told me.

I didn't. I didn't want to be back in my circle. I wanted to be near the memory, even though Joy was trying to eject it.

The memory wouldn't come loose. It stayed put and it stayed sad, and Riley got more and more upset as she thought about it. All the other Emotions got worried because Riley sounded like she was about to cry, and the kids in her class started whispering about her, but was it really so bad that they knew Riley was unhappy? I didn't think so.

As the other Emotions tried to remove the memory from the projector, I walked over to the console and began driving. That's when a new memory sphere was created. It was a bright blue memory of that very moment, and it rolled into Headquarters and toward the core memory holder.

It was a core memory. A sad core memory. I'd made a core memory of my very own.

"No, wait . . ." Joy said. "Stop it . . . no! Aaah!"

She ran to the core memory holder and popped it up so my core memory bounced off the edge and wouldn't go in. But it was supposed to be there. What Joy had done wasn't fair. Then Joy tried to vacuum up the memory, but that would have been even less right. Joy might not have liked the memory, but it was a real core memory. She couldn't just vacuum it away.

"Joy, no," I tried to stop her. I grabbed the memory. "That's a core memory!"

"Hey! Stop it!" Joy said as she tried to pull it away from me.

As we were playing tug-of-war with the blue

core memory, we bumped into the open core memory holder and all five of the yellow core memories tumbled to the ground.

Everyone gasped, and while Joy raced around for the five yellow core memories, I grabbed my blue one. It was special to me, and I wanted it where it belonged, in the holder. But then Joy lunged for it, and it slipped out of my hands and into the vacuum tube. I tried to get it again, but Joy tried to block me, and then she tripped, and then the core memories spilled out of her arms. It was all really confusing. One minute Joy and I were fighting over the core memories, and the next minute those memories, plus Joy and myself, were sucked up into the vacuum tube.

It was very disorienting for a while then. I was in the tube, I was moving quickly . . . and then I fell and landed right beside Joy.

Joy immediately got up and began scrambling around. She was looking for her core memories, I guess, and she found all five. Then she looked around to see where we were.

SADNESS

"Long Term Memory," she said.

I followed her gaze. We were close to Goofball Island, but it was dark and silent. All the Personality Islands would be dark now, because the core memories that powered them weren't in their holder. "This is bad," I said.

But Joy said she could fix everything. We just had to get back to Headquarters, plug in the core memories, and Riley would be back to normal.

If only it could be that easy. Then something horrible dawned on me. Since Joy wasn't in Headquarters, there was no way Riley could be happy! "We gotta get you back up there," I told Joy.

We headed for the bridge to Goofball Island. From there we could cross the lightline back to Headquarters. But once we got to Goofball and took a look at that very thin lightline that spanned across the deep abyss of the Memory Dump, we had second thoughts about our plan. "If we fall, we'll be forgotten forever!" I told Joy.

"We have to do this, for Riley. Just follow my footsteps," Joy said.

It was like walking on a tightrope! I just knew something bad was going to happen. Joy was going to drop one of the core memories, or I was going to stumble and fall into the Memory Dump myself. I've never had good balance. I usually trip over my own feet and land on my face. That's why I just lie down flat on my face on my own. I keep myself from falling that way.

And sure enough, something bad *did* happen. As we were walking along the lightline, I heard a terrible noise, and then Goofball Island and the lightline that we were standing on began to crumble!

"Go back! Run!" yelled Joy.

We raced as fast as we could back across the bridge. We made it back to the Long Term Memory cliff seconds before all of Goofball Island collapsed into the Memory Dump.

"We lost Goofball Island. That means Riley can lose Friendship, and Hockey, and Honesty, and Family! You can fix this, right Joy?" I asked.

"I don't know," Joy replied. "But we have to try."

She then came up with a new plan. The sky had just become dark, which meant Riley had just gone to sleep. That would give us time to walk to Friendship Island and cross the lightline from there. But I looked out at Friendship Island and knew we'd never make it. It was impossible. I wanted to give up and fall on the ground.

"No, no, no, don't obsess over the weight of life's problems," Joy told me.

But it was too late. I fell flat on my face.

"Uhhh, Sadness, we don't have time for this," Joy said as she walked toward the winding Long Term Memory shelves. She was going to walk through Long Term to get to Friendship Island.

"Wait! Joy, you could get lost in there!" I cried.

"Think positive!" she said.

I was thinking positive. I was positive that she was going to get lost in there. I knew from all those mind manuals I read back in Headquarters that Long Term was just one endless warren of corridors and shelves. When I told Joy about the mind manuals and how I knew the way back to

Driven By Emotions

Headquarters, she got really excited. She called me the "Official Mind Map."

"I wish I had a name like that!" said Joy. "How does it feel?"

"Good."

Joy told me to lead the way. And I was going to, but there was just one problem. I was too sad to walk. I needed at least a few hours to pull myself out of my downward spiral.

Apparently, Joy couldn't wait that long. She grabbed one of my legs and dragged me into the maze of Long Term Memory shelves. It actually felt kind of nice, especially since I could run my hand along the bottom row of memories as I slid past them. They turned a really pretty shade of blue when I touched them. I liked it a lot, but I was glad Joy was facing forward and couldn't see. I didn't think she'd approve.

"Which way?" Joy asked when we came to a crossing. "Left?"

"Right."

She turned right.

SADNESS

"No, I mean go left," I told her. "I said left was right. Like 'correct.'"

"Okay! Here we go. This is working!" said Joy, enthusiastic as always.

But then hours passed . . .

"This is not working," she said.

I continued giving her directions. "Just another right . . . and a left. Then another left . . . and a right . . ."

"Are you sure you know where we're going? Because we seem to be walking away from Headquarters—"

Joy paused and looked up. The sky was bright again, which meant Riley was awake. She was distracted for a moment and dropped the core memories. My immediate reaction was to reach out for them.

"Ah, ah, ah, don't touch, remember?" Joy told me. "If you touch them, they stay sad!"

"Oh, sorry, I won't," I said.

Then Joy noticed the long trail of blue memory spheres on the bottom row of all the shelves we had passed. "Ugh, I can't take more of this," she muttered.

Then Joy heard some voices and she ran off. I knew from my manual reading that the voices belonged to Forgetters. Those are the Mind Workers who go through the Long Term Memory shelves and send all the memories Riley doesn't need anymore down to the dump, where the memories fade away forever. That was sad to think about, so I let Joy go to the Forgetters on her own. But when I heard a loud, terrible noise, I got up and walked toward it. Joy had done the same thing. I found her staring out past the Long Term Memory shelves to the place where Friendship Island was breaking into pieces and toppling to the ground.

"Oh, Riley loved that one. And now it's gone," I said. "Good-bye friendship, hello loneliness."

Joy pointed to Hockey Island, which was the closest island, even though it was very far away. "We'll just have to go the long way."

"Yeah," I agreed. "The long . . . long . . . long . . . long way. I'm ready."

I got back down on the floor and lifted my leg so she could drag me, but then Joy ran off again. I found her talking to a strange-looking guy with a trunk, whiskers, and paws. I recognized him. He was Bing Bong, Riley's old imaginary friend, but there was something I had never understood about him.

"What are you supposed to be?" I asked.

"You know," Bing Bong answered, "it's unclear. I'm part cat . . . part elephant . . . part dolphin."

Bing Bong seemed nice. He gave Joy a bag to help her carry the core memories. And he was willing to help us get to Headquarters. He thought we should take the Train of Thought, which sounded like a smart idea since it went up to Headquarters all the time.

"I know a shortcut," he said. "Come on, this way!"

We followed him, but I didn't like the idea of a shortcut. It sounded risky.

Bing Bong led Joy and me to a warehouse. We could see through a door all the way to a window on the building's other side. The train station was right outside that window.

"The station is right through here," Bing Bong said. He opened the door. "After you."

"Joy!" I cried, stopping her.

"What?"

"I read about this place in the manual," I told her. "We shouldn't go in there, that's a bad idea."

"Bing Bong says it's the quickest way to Headquarters," said Joy.

"No, this is Abstract Thought," I explained. "Let's go around. This way," I said, pulling Joy's arm.

"What are you talking about?" Bing Bong asked. "I go in here all the time. It's a shortcut, you see?" He pointed to a sign above the door and spelled it out. "D-A-N-G-E-R, 'shortcut.' I'll prove it to you."

I was pretty sure he hadn't spelled "shortcut," but he went inside and Joy followed, so I went in, too. I didn't like it, though. And I liked it even less when the lights popped on and shapes floated off the floor and into space.

"Say," Bing Bong said, "would you look at that."

"Oh, no," I said, realizing someone must have just activated the room.

I looked over at Bing Bong. His face had turned weird-looking. Like a dream version of his face. Joy and I both screamed, which made Bing Bong touch his face and realize what had happened.

"My face!" he wailed. "My beautiful face!"

"What is going on?" Joy cried.

I told her. "We're abstracting! There are four stages. This is the first: nonobjective fragmentation!"

We tried to walk across the building, but we didn't have joints anymore, so it was pretty hard.

"All right, do not panic!" Bing Bong advised. "What is important is that we all *stay together!*"

Then his arm fell off. Joy's head fell off next. Then I lost my leg. I toppled after it.

"We're in the second stage," I pointed out. "We're deconstructing!"

"Ah!" Bing Bong screamed. "Run!"

I don't like running, but I would have. It was just difficult when we didn't have all of our body parts.

"We've gotta get out of here before we're nothing but shape and color and get stuck here forever!" I cried.

"Stuck?" Joy wailed. "Why did we come in here?"

"I told you," Bing Bong said, "it's a shortcut!"

Through the window, we saw the Train of Thought pull into the station . . . just as we popped into flat, colored shapes.

"Oh, no," I moaned. "We're two-dimensional! That's stage three!"

"Depth!" Bing Bong cried. "I'm lacking depth!"

We still tried to make it to the window, but it was so hard.

"We're getting nowhere!" Joy cried.

Then we abstracted into blobs.

"Oh, no!" I groaned. "We're nonfigurative. This is the last stage!"

"We're not going to make it!" Bing Bong declared.

I was too sad to deal. I slumped to the ground and became a line.

A line! That gave me an idea!

"Wait!" I shouted. "We're two-dimensional. Fall on your face!"

I crawled like an inchworm, and Joy and Bing Bong did the same. As flat lines, we made our way out the far window. We had finally escaped the Abstract Thought building! The bad news was that we had just missed the train, but the good news was that we had popped back to our three-dimensional selves.

"I thought you said that was a shortcut," Joy said to Bing Bong.

"I did, but wow, we should *not* have gone in there," Bing Bong admitted. "That was dangerous! They really should put up a sign."

Bing Bong explained that there was another train station on the other side of Imagination Land. Joy wasn't so sure about his navigation skills after he brought us through Abstract Thought, though, so she turned to me and whispered, "Is there really another station?"

I remembered from the mind manuals that

there was another station. "Uh-huh, through there," I replied.

So we followed Bing Bong into Imagination Land. He was really excited to give us a tour. Joy loved it, but it was a little too strenuous and interactive for me. We had to tromp through French Fry Forest, and Trophy Town, and Cloud Town . . . it really would have been nicer to lie down for a while. Then Bing Bong led us to Preschool World, but on the way there, we heard a loud sound.

It was Hockey Island, crumbling like an iceberg.

"Bing Bong," Joy said, "we have to go back to the station now."

"Sure thing," Bing Bong said. "This way, just past Graham Cracker Castle."

I was pretty sure he was still leading us to Preschool World, not the train station—but then he stopped, like he was confused, too.

"Hey, that's weird," he said. "Graham Cracker Castle used to be right here. I wonder why they moved it?"

He looked around, and seemed to get even

more confused. "Wow, that's not . . . I would have sworn Sparkle Pony Mountain was right here. Hey, what's going on?"

I noticed a bulldozer in front of us. It knocked over a big pink castle.

"Princess Dream World!" Bing Bong gasped.

Glitter dust plumed everywhere. The bulldozer kept moving. "Oh, no!" Bing Bong gasped again. "The Stuffed Animal Hall of Fame!"

The dozer ripped the head off a big stuffed bear. *Sad.* Then Bing Bong saw something that really got him upset.

"My rocket!" he screamed.

It was a wagon, really, and two Forgetters were carrying it toward the pile in front of the bulldozer, which was pushing it all toward the edge of a cliff. Bing Bong ran as fast as he could and tried to catch up with them, but he didn't make it. The Forgetters threw the rocket on the pile, and the bulldozer shoved it and the rest of the rubble off a cliff and into the dump.

"Nooo!" he protested. "No! No! No! You can't

take my rocket to the dump! Riley and I are going to the *moon!*"

But the rocket was gone. Bing Bong was so stunned and distraught he dropped to his knees. "Riley can't be done with me."

Joy walked over to him and tried to make him feel better. "Hey, it's going to be okay!" she said. "We can fix this! We just need to get back to Headquarters. Which way to the train station?"

She tried to lead him back, but Bing Bong wouldn't move. "I had a whole trip planned for us," he said.

Joy tried again. "Hey, who's ticklish, huh? Here comes the tickle monster . . ."

She tickled him, but he didn't respond.

"Hey, Bing Bong!" Joy tried. "Look at this!"

She made a silly face. He didn't even glance at her. I could tell Joy was getting impatient.

"Here's a fun game!" she said. "You point to the train station and we all go there! Won't that be fun? Come on, let's go to the train station!"

I understood Joy wanted to get back to

Headquarters. I did, too. But Bing Bong didn't need someone to cheer him up or get him motivated. He was sad because something really depressing had happened to him.

He *needed* to be sad.

I sat down next to him. "I'm sorry they took your rocket," I said. "They took something that you loved. It's gone . . . forever."

"Sadness, don't make him feel worse," Joy said.

"Sorry," I said . . . but I wasn't. Not really. I didn't want to upset Joy, but I thought, well, maybe she just didn't understand.

Bing Bong still stared into the pit where his rocket had disappeared. "It's all I had left of Riley," he said.

"I bet you and Riley had great adventures," I told him.

"They were wonderful," Bing Bong agreed. "Once we flew back in time. We had breakfast twice that day."

"That sounds amazing," I said. "I bet Riley liked it."

"Oh, she did," Bing Bong said. "We were best friends."

He started to cry then. He cried candy, just the way Riley imagined he would when she was little. I let him put his head on my shoulder.

"Yeah, it's sad," I said.

I put my arm around him and let him cry. Eventually, the sobs got softer . . . then slower . . . and then they turned to sniffles. He lifted his head and blinked, wiping at his eyes.

"I'm okay now," he said. "C'mon, the train station is this way."

He started walking. I felt tired, like I'd been crying, too, but I also felt good, because I'd made it better for Bing Bong. I got up so I could follow him, but Joy was in front of me, and she had this weird look on her face.

"Wow," she said. "How did you do that?"

"I don't know," I admitted. "He was sad. So I listened—"

Suddenly, we heard the train whistle.

"Hey!" Bing Bong shouted. "There's the train!"

I hurried to catch up with him, and soon he, Joy, and I were riding the Train of Thought. It was a nice ride, but when it became nighttime and things got dark, the train stopped.

"Hey, hey!" Joy called to the engineer. "Why aren't we moving?"

"Riley's gone to sleep," the engineer said. "We're all on break."

"You mean we're stuck here until morning?" I asked.

"Yeah," Bing Bong noted. "The Train of Thought doesn't run while she's asleep."

"Oh, we can't wait that long!" Joy cried.

"How about we wake her up?" I suggested.

"Sadness, that's ridiculous," Joy scolded me. "How could we possibly . . ." Then she spotted the gates to Dream Productions. Her face lit up like she had an amazing idea. "How about we wake her up!"

"Great idea, Joy," I said.

"Thanks," she said. "Come on!"

We walked to Dream Productions, where they

produce Riley's dreams. Once we were through the gate, we were surrounded by lots of actors in costumes, set workers and lighting guys, and lots of people on golf carts. Everyone seemed very busy.

"Whoa!" Joy marveled. "This place is huge."

"Yeah," I said, "it looks so much smaller than I expected."

Joy got really excited when she saw a unicorn sitting in a director's chair, so I went up to it and said, "My friend says you're famous. She wants your autograph."

Joy didn't like that. "No, no, Sadness, don't bother Miss Unicorn, okay?"

It was like she was embarrassed or something. Oh, well.

Joy, Bing Bong, and I got to a big building: STAGE B. It seemed like a good place to find the Dream Productions team, so we went inside. There was a lot going on—lots of actors and sets and props and things. We weren't supposed to be inside, so we hid behind some production equipment and shuffled over to a rack of costumes.

"Okay, how are we gonna wake her up?" Joy asked.

"Well," I said, "she wakes up sometimes when she has a scary dream. We could scare her."

"Scare her?" Joy echoed. "No, no, she's been through enough already. Sadness, you may know your way around down here, but I know Riley! We're gonna make her so happy she'll wake up with exhilaration! We'll excite her awake!"

"That's never happened before," I noted.

"Ooh!" Joy squealed as she found a costume she liked. "Riley loves dogs. Put this on!"

It was the back half of a dog costume. Joy took the front half.

"I don't think that'll work," I warned her, but I put on the costume anyway. Then Joy and I stood to the side of the set while everyone started shooting the dream. It was a dream about Riley's first day at school, except even sadder than the way it actually happened. She was talking to her whole class . . . but then her teeth fell out and it turned out she wasn't wearing pants.

"Ready?" Joy asked me.

"I don't think this happy thing is going to work," I said. "But if we scare her—"

"Here we go!" yelled Joy.

She pulled me out with her, which was pretty easy since she was the front half of the dog, and we tried to leap around like a puppy. I guess it went okay. I couldn't see anything from my part of the costume. All I knew was Joy was barking and running around for a long time, and still no one shouted that Riley was waking up, so I knew it wasn't working. I said so to Joy, but before she could answer me, the costume split in half. I thought that might be good and scary, so I ran away from Joy, all around the classroom set.

"Huh?" Joy whispered. "Sadness, what are you doing? Come back here!"

I saw Bing Bong jump in front of the camera, so I let Joy get closer to me.

"Sadness!" she said accusingly. "You are ruining this dream! You're scaring her!"

"But look," I said, "it's working!"

I pointed to the Sleep Indicator on the wall. It was moving from ASLEEP to AWAKE. It wasn't there yet, but it was a lot closer than when we started. Being half-dogs was a lot more effective than being one full dog. I wanted to have Joy actually catch my tail in her mouth and shake it around while I whimpered, but we didn't get the chance.

"*THEY ARE NOT PART OF THIS DREAM!*" the director yelled. "*GET THEM!*"

Security came to get us. Joy and I left the dream and ran away, but they got Bing Bong. We couldn't help him, because if they saw us, they'd grab us, too. Joy was really upset because Bing Bong had been holding the bag of core memories for her, and now they were gone, too.

I saw where they took him. It was the Subconscious. To get there and find him, Joy and I had to go down a massive, dark, spooky staircase. At the bottom was a giant gate, with only darkness and eerie noises behind it. The gate was watched by two guards.

"What is this place?" Joy whispered.

"The Subconscious," I told her. "I read about it in the manual. It's where they take all the troublemakers."

Joy looked at the guards. "Hmmm. How do we get in?"

I had an idea. I motioned for Joy to follow me. The two guards were deep in conversation, so Joy and I just tiptoed past them. We walked right up to the closed gate . . . then I shook it.

"Hey! You!" one guard shouted.

"Oh! You caught us!" I said. I tried to sound really guilty.

"Get back in there!" the other guard demanded. "No escaping!"

The guards shoved Joy and me through the gate and then slammed it shut.

I'd gotten us inside, but the place was really a massive, dark, damp cave with noises that echoed in spooky ways. "I don't like it here," I told Joy. "It's where they keep Riley's darkest fears."

"It's broccoli!" Joy gasped as she saw a giant stalk of the evil vegetable. Then a door in the rock wall creaked open, revealing a rickety set of stairs. Joy and I both screamed.

"The stairs to the basement!" I yelled.

And we'd only just gotten away from them when we heard a giant roar and a massive vacuum cleaner popped out of the shadows and came after us.

"Grandma's vacuum cleaner!" Joy screamed.

We ran until it was out of sight, then hid behind a rock. Once we'd caught our breath, we tried tiptoeing through the cave again. We tried to be very quiet, but every step I took crunched down on something.

"Would you walk quieter?" Joy asked.

"I'm trying!" I told her.

"What is going—" Joy asked, reaching down and picking something up. "Candy wrappers."

Bing Bong cried candy, so it seemed like a good sign. We followed the trail of wrappers. Soon we heard sobbing.

"Bing Bong!" Joy cried.

He was there, crouched down in a big cage

made of balloons. He seemed happy to see us for about a second; then he warned us to be very quiet. He pointed, and we realized we were right next to a giant sleeping clown.

"It's Jangles," Joy said. She sounded terrified. Jangles scared me, too. Riley met Jangles at her cousin's birthday party. He had a face white as a tomb and a grinning mouth so red it looked like he snacked on children. I'm pretty sure his teeth were fangs, too. All of them.

This Jangles was even scarier than the real one. He was as big as a T. rex. And he murmured wickedly while he slept. "Who's the birthday girl?" he slurred.

Joy spoke very softly. "Do you still have the core memories?"

"Yeah." Bing Bong handed them through the balloon-cage slats and Joy slung the bag back over her shoulder. "All he cared about was the candy!"

Joy tried to pry apart the balloons so Bing Bong could get out, but they squeaked like fingernails running down a blackboard and made the hair on my neck stand up. I watched to see if Jangles would wake up. He snorted and rolled over, but stayed asleep as Joy stretched the bars even farther and Bing Bong escaped.

"We're out of here!" Bing Bong declared. "Let's get to that train and wait for morning."

We were running really fast, but then Joy stopped and grabbed my arm. "Wait, the train's not running. We still have to wake up Riley."

"But how?" I asked.

We both had the same idea at once. We looked up at Jangles.

"Oh, no," said Bing Bong.

Joy and I gathered all our courage and woke up Jangles. We told him that there was going to be a birthday party. That was enough to get him really excited.

The three of us ran to the gates of the Subconscious with Jangles right behind us. He destroyed the big gate with his mallet, and the guards were so scared they ran away. That left us free to run back up the big stairway to Dream

Productions, where they were still shooting Riley's dream.

Jangles rammed down the studio wall with his mallet, then leaned into the camera and grinned. *"WHO'S THE BIRTHDAY GIRL?!"* he roared.

I peeked around him and saw the Sleep Indicator go all the way to AWAKE. It worked! Joy and I were so happy we did a little dance. Just a short one—dancing makes my feet hurt. Then we ran to the Train of Thought and caught the very last car just as it was pulling away.

"Guess who's on their way to Headquarters?!" Joy cried. She grabbed me and spun me around, which was fun, but it made me a little dizzy. I still liked it, though.

"We are!" I replied. I could see Headquarters up in the distance. It was still pretty far, but the train would get us there. In the meantime, we were surrounded by all the memories in the train car, and that was nice. Especially for Bing Bong. He hadn't spent time with Riley in a while, so he liked looking at her memories.

SADNESS

"Hey, that was a good idea," Joy said to me. "About scaring Riley awake. You're not so bad."

I wasn't sure, but it sounded like Joy was saying something nice to me. "Really?" I asked.

"Nice work," said Joy.

I smiled. I had done good. And Joy thought so, too. She'd never liked anything I'd done before. I felt kind of warm and fuzzy inside.

Then Bing Bong showed us a memory sphere he'd found. In it, Riley's hockey teammates were holding her in the air. Joy smiled because she said she loved this one.

"Yeah," I said. "I love that one, too."

That made Joy happy. "Atta girl!" she cried. "Now you're getting it!"

"Yeah," I sighed. "It was the day the Prairie Dogs lost the big play-off game. Riley missed the winning shot. She felt awful. She wanted to quit."

Joy looked disappointed.

"Sorry. I can't help it," I said. I had really thought Joy finally liked me, and now she didn't all over again.

"I'll tell ya what," said Joy, smiling. "We'll keep working on it together. Okay?"

"Okay," I said. I promised myself I would, and I'd work hard on it, too. Then Joy would be happier with me. I saw Joy put the memory in her bag with the core memories and thought maybe I'd look at it again later and try to see it the way she did.

All of a sudden, we heard a terrible noise and the whole train shuddered. We looked around. Honesty Island was sinking! And it was ruining the train tracks! They toppled, and the train plummeted down. It happened too fast for me to be scared; I was just sad I wouldn't have the time to practice being positive like I'd promised Joy.

We crashed into the Long Term Memory cliffs, right at the edge of a steep drop-off. The train slipped down and crashed into the dump, but Joy, Bing Bong, and I were able to cling to the ledge and scramble up. We looked down and saw the train falling farther and farther away.

"That was our way home!" Joy wailed. "We lost another island . . . what is happening?"

A Mind Worker answered. "Haven't you heard? Riley is running away."

Running away? That was the saddest news I had ever heard. We had to do something about it.

"Joy," I said, "if we hurry, we can still stop her."

"Family Island," Joy said. "Let's go!"

She was right. Family Island was the last one left. If we got there, we could make our way to Headquarters. We ran across the bridge to the island, but it started to shake and crumble.

"Joy!" I cried, trying to stop her before she went too far ahead. "Joy! It's too dangerous! We won't make it in time!"

"But that's our only way back!" she shouted.

Actually, it wasn't. At that moment, one of the shelves in Long Term broke, exposing a recall tube that sent memories back up to Headquarters.

"We can get recalled!" I said.

As we ran toward the tube, Family Island rumbled and a huge chunk of it broke off. The bridge and part of the cliff's edge crumbled and fell into the Memory Dump. We had to act fast.

Driven By Emotions

"Go!" Joy screamed. "Run! RUN!"

Joy made it to the recall tube first. After she entered it, I stepped in beside her.

"Whoa, whoa!" she snapped. "Sadness, stop! You are hurting Riley!"

I didn't know what she meant. Then she pulled out one of the core memories. It was bright blue because I'd leaned against it.

I felt horrible. I hadn't tried to change the core memories. They hadn't even called to me the way they had the first time I'd changed one. I didn't understand what was happening, but I knew I was disappointing Joy . . . and she said I was hurting Riley, too.

I would never hurt Riley. Not on purpose.

The cliffs underneath us were starting to crumble. If we were going to get recalled, we had to move now. I wasn't sure how I'd squeeze in next to Joy without touching the core memories, but there had to be some way.

Then I realized the tube was already coming down and closing over Joy. She held her bag of core memories tightly and rode up the tube alone. All I could do was watch her go.

"Joy?" I called hopelessly.

Bing Bong called after her, too, but she was already on her way.

She'd left us. But at least she'd get to back to Headquarters and help Riley. That was the most important thing.

The ground shook harder underneath us. More of the cliff was falling away. I scrambled back so I wouldn't fall. I didn't realize the shaking was affecting Joy's recall tube . . . but Bing Bong did. As a huge chunk of the ground fell away and crumbled down to the dump, I hid my face in my arms. When I looked up, I was at the very edge of a brand-new, very steep cliff. My ears were ringing, but I still heard something that sounded like screams.

I peered over the cliff's edge. When I looked down, I saw Joy and Bing Bong, far, far away, and still plummeting down to the abyss.

"Joy!" I screamed, but she was too far to hear me. I sat back and buried my face in my hands.

Even though I knew she couldn't hear me, I spoke to her. "I'm sorry."

I don't know how long I sat there. I tried for a while to shout down to Joy and Bing Bong, but I never heard anything back. I knew from the manuals that the dump was very deep below the surface of Long Term Memory. Worse, I knew what happened to anything that landed in the dump. It faded away, forgotten forever. Thanks to me, that's what would happen to Joy and Bing Bong . . . and Riley's core memories.

Joy was right. I was hurting Riley. I'd *hurt* Riley. If I hadn't started touching memories . . . if I'd just listened to Joy and stayed in my Circle of Sadness, none of this would have happened.

I wished I was the one who was about to disappear. Part of me wanted to throw myself into the dump, but I couldn't do it. Still, I knew a place where I *could* disappear. A place so big and vast and winding that no one would ever find me.

I trudged slowly to the maze of Long Term Memory shelves. I walked inside . . . and kept

SADNESS

walking. I think I dragged my hand along a shelf. I might have touched memories. I might have turned them blue. I don't really know. I didn't feel anything. I just walked. If I could have, I'd have walked forever.

Once I heard that when people are depressed, they can hear things in their heads. That must have been what happened to me, because at one point, I heard Joy's voice behind me.

"Sadness!" she cried.

I sighed. It was just my imagination. Joy was gone.

But when I heard the voice again, I turned around. She was there. Joy was there!

"Joy?" I asked.

For the littlest second, I was excited . . . but then I knew that if Joy had made it back from the dump, she needed to get back to Headquarters *without me*. I would only ruin everything, just like I had from the beginning. I ran as fast as I could away from her.

"Wait, Sadness!" Joy yelled.

She chased me. It was nice she wanted me around, but I knew I shouldn't turn back.

"You were right, Joy," I called to her. "Riley's better off without me!"

I ran and ran, turning corners whenever I could so I would lose Joy, but I still heard her pounding after me. I left the Long Term Memory shelves and ran into Imagination Land. I ducked into the French Fry Forest and toppled fries into her path so she couldn't follow me, but she got past them. In Cloud Town I grabbed a chunk of cloud and tried to float away.

"Sadness!" Joy called after me.

I couldn't let her catch me. I was high above her and moving fast. I'd get away, then Joy and Riley and everyone else would be safe.

I'd flown pretty far, and I was getting used to the idea of flying around aimlessly for the rest of my life, when something whapped into me.

"Joy?" I asked, surprised.

She'd been the thing that whapped into me. I don't know how she got into the air, but she did, and she'd grabbed me, and now we were zooming across the sky, and . . .

SPLAT!

We smashed into the side of Headquarters and slid down the window. We almost fell, but we both managed to grab hold of the window ledge. We held on tight.

I wanted to ask Joy how she got to me. I wanted to tell her she shouldn't have done it, that everyone was better off with me not around . . . but it took all my energy just to hold on.

Joy managed to pull herself higher. She banged on the window. I saw Fear, Anger, and Disgust appear on the other side. They shouted some things, but I couldn't hear what they said. Then I saw flame, and a circle of glass was sliced out of the window. Fear, Disgust, and Anger leaned out through the hole and helped Joy and me inside.

I almost cried. It felt so good to be back in Headquarters, but at the same time, I knew it was the last place I should be. On the big screen, I saw Riley sitting on a bus. She was all by herself, and the bus was moving. She was running away, just like we'd heard. I hoped Joy could take care of it.

Instead, she turned to me. "Sadness," she said, "it's up to you."

I was sure I heard her wrong, but she kept looking at me. "Me?" I asked. "I can't, Joy."

"Riley needs you," she said.

Riley . . . needed me?

I could tell from the look on Joy's face that she believed it.

Riley had lost so much. Her home, her friends, her hockey team . . . everything that was familiar to her.

Riley *should* be sad about all that. She *needed* to be.

I took the console and steered.

There was an idea bulb that was sparking and steaming, but it flicked off when I put my hands on the controls. I removed it and placed it aside.

Riley's face started to look sad. She thought for a little bit, then she jumped up.

"Wait!" Riley told the driver. "Stop!"

The driver did. Riley ran to the front.

"I wanna get off," she said.

I kept steering as she ran away from the bus, all the way home. Her new home. When she walked in, Mom and Dad rushed over to her.

"Riley!" Mom cried.

"Riley, there you are!" Dad echoed. "Thank goodness!"

"We were worried sick!" Mom said. "Where have you been? It's so late . . ."

They looked so upset. Riley had worried them so much . . . I knew they really loved her to get that worried about her.

"Honey, what happened?" Dad asked Riley. "Are you all right?"

"We asked the neighbors, we called the school, I talked to your teacher . . ." Mom added.

I needed a way for Riley to show her parents how she really felt, but I wasn't sure what to do. Then Joy handed me all the core memories. She *wanted* me to touch them. I met her eyes—was she sure? Joy nodded.

Driven By Emotions

I touched them all until they become completely blue. I placed one in the recall unit so Riley could remember it. It was a memory of her and her best friend, Meg, laughing together when they were really little.

Riley cried as she remembered it. One by one, I put the blue core memories into the recall unit so Riley could think about them. Each one made her cry more, but that was okay. It was good.

Finally, she was ready to speak to her parents.

"I know you don't want me to," she sobbed, "but I miss home. I miss Minnesota. You need me to be happy, but . . . I want my old friends back, and my hockey team. I wanna go home. Please don't be mad."

"We're not mad," Dad said. "You know what? I miss Minnesota, too. I miss the woods where we took hikes."

"And the backyard where you used to play," Mom added.

"Spring Lake, where you learned to skate," Dad said.

Their memories made Riley cry even more, but it felt good, like a relief. Soon they were all hugging and crying and sharing the memories they'd always love . . . but always miss, too.

Joy reached into her satchel and handed me something I didn't know she had: my blue core memory. The one Riley had made when she spoke in front of the class.

I took Joy's hand and put it on the console. Now we were running things together. On the screen, we saw Riley smile through her tears. Then something wonderful happened. A new core memory was formed! It was a combination of joy and sadness, both yellow and blue. It rolled into the core memory holder and created a brand-new Family Island.

So on that day, Joy and I became a team.

A lot changed after that. It's been a bunch of months, and Riley's happy in San Francisco now. She's sad sometimes, too, and sometimes she's angry, scared, or disgusted. But most of the time she's a mix of all of us. That's why we have an

Driven By Emotions

improved console—a big one that we can all drive at once. The view out Headquarters' windows is pretty nice, too. Riley has brand-new Islands of Personality, including Tragic Vampire Romance Island, which I just can't get enough of!

Things are good. And when they're not good that's good, too.

And I don't feel left out anymore. We're all in this together, and we're all looking out for Riley. She's twelve now, and Joy thinks everything will be smooth from here on out.

I don't have the heart to tell her otherwise.

SADNESS

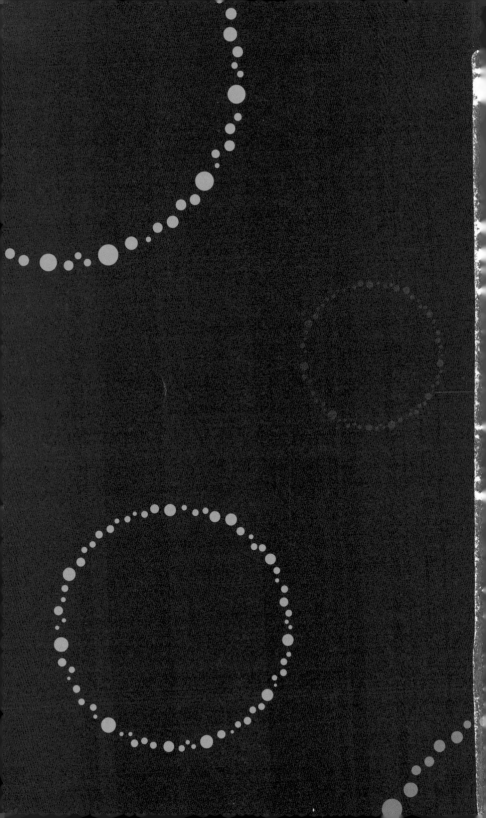